MOON OVER HANKS HOLLOW

HANKS HOLLOW SERIES BOOK ONE

RACHELLE KAMPEN

To Aaron and Annie. You both give me so much love and support. I love you so much.

PROLOGUE

Thunder rumbled ominously in the distance as Simon Hart climbed out of his jet-black Range Rover and stared up at Hart House. The impending storm added a green hue to the fading light of dusk. An unsettling end to an unsettling day.

Simon climbed polished steps leading to an expansive stone veranda, and the heavy oak front door swung open as he approached. Four members of his pack emerged, their postures stiff, anxiously awaiting Simon's news.

"I met with the other alphas." Simon squared his shoulders.

His pack stared back at him with eyes matching his own. The red-brown hue was a trait shared by all the Hart family members. His six-and-a-half-foot frame towered over the others.

"We're all in agreement. This needs to go to the Council."

"It should never have gotten this far." Frank spat the words, seething. "You should have terminated the pregnancy the second you found out what it was. It's an abomination brought into this world by witchcraft."

Simon faced his cousin and growled. Disrespecting the alpha came with repercussions, but Frank didn't seem to care. Ever since Simon was chosen as alpha by Frank's late grandfather, Frank walked around with a grudge that teetered on hatred.

"Watch how you're speaking to your alpha, *pup*," Stuart scolded. His bushy gray eyebrows furrowed in a disapproving stare. Stuart's tired old frame wasn't the least bit intimidating, but Simon appreciated his uncle's loyalty.

"Watch who you're calling a pup, *old man*," Frank shot back, puffing his chest and stepping toward Stuart. With an unruly black mop of hair and a perpetual five o'clock shadow, he always looked a bit wild, but now his eyes glowed yellow.

Frank's twin brother, Amos, stood back, his eyes nervously flitting between the pack members. Though identical, Frank was unkempt while Amos's neatness bordered on obsessive. Always clean-shaven and impeccably dressed, he was stiff and proper.

"Back off, Frank." Jack, Stuart's son, maneuvered between the two men and nudged Frank away. Jack wasn't a fighter, but he wouldn't let anyone intimidate his dad. He glared at Frank, daring him to push back.

"Enough!" Simon's voice sliced through the air, and the pack stilled. "I requested an audience with the Council. I'll leave for Alaska in the morning."

"Did you bother to tell the other alphas the woman you impregnated was a witch?" Frank's sneer tested Simon's patience, which was wearing thinner by the moment.

"I did not tell them she was a witch, and I won't tell the

Council she was a witch." Simon kept his voice level. "It's not true. You're delusional."

Amos, who'd been quiet up until this point, cleared his throat and cautioned, "Simon, think about this. If you take this to the Council, they may decide it's best to let the child live. They'll force you to raise it."

Amos had always been more diplomatic than his brother, but Simon wasn't fooled. He knew Amos was just as much of a self-righteous prick as Frank. The twins were a walking, talking pair of jackasses. Just like their father, they wanted to keep up traditions—the old-fashioned way of doing things. They hated change and progress and everything that came with it.

"I'm counting on it," Simon growled. "*It* is my daughter, and I plan to ask—to *beg*—the Council to let her live as one of the pack."

"You've lost your mind!" Frank yelled, his face reddening. He clenched his fists at his sides. "In all the centuries of our existence, there has never been a female werewolf." He turned toward the other members of the pack, desperate for backup. "Our alpha isn't himself. He's bewitched by that whore."

A red haze of fury took hold of Simon, and his body vibrated with the need to shift. "Watch yourself, Frank. Gwen died bringing my child into this world, and I will not listen to you disrespect her."

"Good riddance," Frank spat as he advanced on Simon. "She was a witch, and her child is a witch. They both need to die, and you know it."

The last tendrils of Simon's control snapped, and his body exploded forward, morphing into an enormous wolf. Gray and black markings peppered the white coat covering his giant frame. His eyes glowed with a fierceness that pierced the night, his large fangs bared in fury. Snarling, Simon lunged at Frank, knocking him off the front porch and onto the lawn. Instead of giving deference to his alpha and backing down, Frank reciprocated, leaping to his feet and shifting to wolf form. His sleek black coat camouflaged him in the darkness of night. His yellow eyes were the only pop of color that gave him away. The two wolves paced in a circle, each daring the other to make the next move.

The remaining pack members jumped off the porch, shifting and surrounding Simon and Frank, recognizing Frank's alpha challenge.

"*Yield, Frank,*" Simon snarled telepathically. His voice sounded as deadly in the pack members' heads as it would if he'd uttered the words verbally in human form.

"*No.*" Frank's voice was firm. "*That child needs to die.*"

Simon sprang forward, vicious anger replacing his usual calm, composed nature. Frank met him midstride, and the two collided in a tangle of limbs, each biting at the other, struggling to find purchase, eager to tear into flesh. Their growls mingled with the rattle of thunder as the storm rolled in.

A bolt of lightning lit the sky, and rain pummeled from black clouds, soaking their fur and wetting the ground into a muddy mess. Stuart and Jack barked and howled, encouraging Simon, while Amos growled nervously for his twin.

Simon quickly gained the upper hand, flinging Frank aside like a filthy rag. Frank rolled across the torn-up grass and lay still, his ribcage heaving with deep, labored breaths. Slowly, he rolled onto all fours. Mud and fresh blood caked his fur. He limped forward with his head held low.

"*I yield.*" Venom laced Frank's telepathic hiss.

Simon stood tall and threw his head up into the rain, releasing a long, low howl. The other wolves joined in, baying with their alpha. Frank lowered himself to the ground in submission.

Simon moved forward and stood over Frank, baring his teeth in a low growl. *"Leave, Frank."*

Frank snapped his head up, a low whimper escaping his throat. *"No. I can't, Simon. I have nowhere else to go."*

"You should have thought about that before you threatened my child. Leave, Frank. Get out. You're banished. You are no longer a member of this pack." He turned toward the others. *"Anyone else have a problem with me?"*

Frank glanced toward his brother, but Amos refused to meet his eyes. He kept his gaze lowered to the ground.

Simon's throat rumbled in another low growl. A warning.

Frank crept past him and slipped away into the rainy darkness of the night.

~

Fresh blossoms lined the path to Clara Magee's front porch. The happy whistles of birds filled the air, and sunlight flooded the garden, where butterflies danced above the flowers. Peace descended over Simon as he drew closer to the front door. He recognized the feeling. He had felt it every time he was with Gwen.

Pretending not to know Gwen was a witch was easiest and made him feel like he wasn't lying to his pack. The truth went unspoken. They all knew what she was.

He missed her so much. He hadn't meant to fall so hard. Love wasn't a good idea for werewolves. For hundreds of years, werewolves hunted only one kind of human—women. They were the mothers of their children and the servants they forced to work in their homes.

Werewolves put on polite smiles in the human world, where females held high-ranking positions and were treated as equals. But in their secret society, behind closed doors, they lived in male-only packs, keeping their existence hidden from the rest of the world.

In recent decades, most werewolves evolved past the brutality of their past to find alternative ways of growing their packs. A surrogate agency was formed, and its popularity was growing rapidly. Most werewolves still kept women as servants, but rather than kidnapping and forced labor, many werewolves sought out lonely, homeless souls, promising a home if they swore themselves to the pack for the rest of their lives.

Of course, the threat of death existed for any human who decided to leave a werewolf's home armed with their secret.

Still, some werewolves clung to the past, still hunting women, brutally enslaving them, and forcing them to bear their offspring. Though the Council didn't condone that, they didn't forbid it either.

Simon's hand lingered over Clara's door for a few moments. What lay on the other side shook the very foundation of the male-dominated world of werewolves.

The United States Werewolf Council had spoken. They conferred with werewolf leaders around the globe, and the consensus—while wrought with controversy—was that they wanted his daughter to live. They wanted to see what happened...what she would become.

The door was flung open before he had a chance to knock.

"Are you going to stand out there all day, brooding like that, or are you coming in?" Clara stared at him, a hand on her hip, her messy dark-gray hair tied on top of her head. Her dress hung loosely over her full, solid frame.

Simon stepped carefully inside, and she shut the door behind him. Though he towered over her, the fierce woman intimidated him. His presence took command of every room he entered...until he entered a room occupied by Clara. From the moment Gwen introduced Simon to her mother, he'd felt like a bug under a microscope. A permanent half grin was etched on Clara's face, like she knew every secret lingering in Simon's head.

When he first met Gwen, avoiding Clara had been easy. He and Gwen would meet in town at Miller's Bar and Grill or at the park in the center of Hanks Hollow. However, when Gwen's pregnancy put her on bedrest, Simon was forced to come to her home and face Clara's furious stares. The woman made no effort to hide her disdain for Simon. She clearly didn't approve of their relationship or Gwen's pregnancy.

When Gwen went into labor, she insisted on a home delivery. She said she would be in better hands with her mother than with any doctor. Simon was reluctant, but he couldn't make Gwen do anything she didn't want to. Nobody could.

When the baby was born, all wrinkly and covered in blood, Clara thrust the infant into his hands as she tended to Gwen. Peeking at the fragile baby he clumsily held in his arms, Simon gasped. He blinked, not believing his eyes.

A daughter. Werewolves didn't have daughters. Werewolves only had sons. He wondered for a moment if Gwen had been unfaithful. The baby couldn't be his. But then he sensed the truth. He could smell the werewolf in the child he held.

He barely had time to ponder the implications when

Clara's screams tore through the air. His beautiful Gwen was dead. The love of his life lay cold and lifeless on the bed, bathed in her own blood.

"Are you back for good this time?" Clara's voice dripped with contempt, snapping Simon back to the present. He shakily exhaled as he ran a hand over his mouth. His eyes stung with tears, and he tried to push the memory to the back of his mind.

He'd left the baby with Clara while he sought answers and guidance from the other alphas and the Council. Now, he was back for his daughter. The Hart pack would be the first in history to raise a female werewolf.

He nodded slowly, and Clara jerked her head once in a single answering nod before wordlessly shuffling into the other room. Simon hesitated before following her, his stomach flipping nervously.

The bedroom that was once Gwen's had been transformed into a makeshift nursery. Boxes of diapers and piles of tiny clothes littered every surface, and a mobile made of branches and dried flowers hung over a small white crib in the corner.

Clara bent over the crib to reach inside. She picked up the bundle, a tiny swath of pink encircled by Clara's unusually large hands. She handed the baby to Simon, and he quickly took hold, afraid she would let go before he was ready. He studied the infant, and a small smile tugged at his lips. A fuzzy tuft of red hair puffed along the top of her wrinkled head. Brown eyes stared up at him, searching his face.

"What's her name?" Clara asked. "I'm tired of calling her Baby."

A name. Simon hadn't thought about a name. The few times he and Gwen talked about the baby, he'd been so sure they were having a boy that he hadn't bothered with girl names.

"What was Gwen's middle name?" he asked suddenly. His cheeks heated under Clara's incredulous stare. He didn't even know her middle name.

She sighed. "Rose."

"Rose." Simon nodded. He eyed the child. She had rosy cheeks and a puff of red hair. It fit. It fit perfectly. Rose Hart.

ONE

ROSIE

THE LARGE OAK TREE AT THE NORTH CORNER OF THE Hart estate served as a grounding place for Rosie. It was where the estate grounds ended and miles upon miles of wild forest began. The tree had been her favorite place to sit for as long as she could remember. There, she had a foot in both worlds. She could stay in touch with the familiarity of her home and her family, but she could also dip her toes into the wilderness and feel its siren call.

The oak was more familiar to her than most people. It stood tall, its branches reaching to the sky, and she drew energy from its strength. The bark was rough, like her father's stubble after a day with no shave, and she craved the feel against her cheek. The rustle of its leaves in the wind had sung her to sleep countless times. Its roots ran deep, reminding her that it had been there much longer than her sixteen years on this earth, holding secrets about the generations of her family who had wandered these grounds before her.

Rosie sat underneath the oak tree just like she did almost every afternoon. All around her, the sounds and smells of the forest prickled her senses. A sudden jolt of excited energy startled her, and she looked to her left, spotting the soft, bushy tail of a young squirrel. Rosie recalled watching the same squirrel and its three siblings a few weeks earlier when they ventured out from their nest for the first time.

"You're getting bigger," Rosie mused.

The squirrel stopped, flaring its nostrils and sniffing the air before it continued scampering up the trunk of the pine tree toward what was left of the nest.

"Where are your brothers?"

The words hadn't even left her mouth when two of the squirrels in question came tearing down the tree. All three of them jumped into the bed of dead leaves on the ground and took off, chasing each other and chirping happily. As they bopped away, leaves from the pile settled, uncovering the fourth squirrel lying still in the dirt. Rosie crawled across the ground to take a closer look, and the squirrel's pain smacked her like a slap in the face. Apparently, the fall from the nest had hurt him badly. He wouldn't live long.

Rosie bit her lip. Despite the constant encouragement from her grandma, she rarely used her power of healing. She'd only used it once on a person. The memory formed like a dark cloud over her head, and she shook it away. After that first time, she hid her healing away from prying eyes, using it only a few times in the forest when she came upon a broken-winged bird or a sick animal.

The squirrel's body shuddered with its breath, and another wave of its agony hit her. She reached forward, the desire to take the squirrel's pain away outweighing her trepidation. A warm current spread through her hand and fingertips, and she gently touched the squirrel's tummy. Energy seeped from her fingers and spread into the tiny body. She flinched as the squirrel flipped itself over onto its feet. It sat still, disoriented, before giving a little shake of its tail then bouncing off through the leaves in search of its siblings.

After crawling back to her resting place at the foot of the oak, Rosie leaned against the rough bark of the trunk. She closed her eyes and breathed in her surroundings, listening to the leaves rustling on the forest floor as the squirrels continued to play.

She cracked her eyes open and stared toward Hart House. The estate had been in her family for generations and was by far one of the oldest properties in Wisconsin. Nestled within several square miles of privately owned forest, a locked gate separated a remote, rarely traveled road from the long tree-lined driveway. The driveway opened to a clearing and looped to the front of a massive house. The house itself was fairly new, built only about twenty years ago atop the foundation of the house that stood there before it. Plenty of room for their pack, with twelve bedrooms—most with their own bathrooms—two kitchens, a formal dining room, a den with a fireplace, a rec room, a living room with another fireplace, and a library.

Flowering trees and neatly trimmed hedges bordered a pristinely manicured lawn in the backyard. The hedges thickened around the gated garden, where flowers bloomed from spring until fall. Beyond the garden, Rosie's oak tree stood sentry at the edge of the forest.

Rosie gave the oak a goodbye pat and was about to head back to the house when she heard two sets of heavy foot-steps approaching.

"Are you hugging trees again, Rosie?" The voice belonged to her older brother, Sam, which meant the other set of footsteps undoubtedly belonged to her best friend, Lucas.

"Come on," Lucas chimed in with a laugh. "She's been hugging this tree since she could walk. The question is, has she gotten her wish? Has the tree started hugging her back yet?"

Rosie rolled her eyes and ground her teeth. "Don't you losers have anything better to do than make fun of me? I came out here to be alone."

The forest was the only place Rosie could explore her gifts and find solitude, yet Lucas and Sam always seemed to find her. She loved them dearly, but sometimes, she needed her space.

Sam's forehead creased. No one at school believed they were brother and sister although technically, they were half siblings. Very few werewolves shared the same mother. While they had the same red-brown eyes, Sam had a tall, muscular build, tan skin, and a head of loose blond curls. Conversely, Rosie was short, scrawny, and pale.

A wave of remorse rolled off them, and Rosie absorbed their emotion like a sponge. Sam and Lucas often teased her about her witch magic. She tolerated it, assuming it was some sort of strange male version of affection. Usually, she laughed along with them, but something had her on edge. Maybe it was the long day she had at school. Or maybe she was getting her period.

"Aw, Rosie. We're sorry," Lucas said, a slight blush tingeing his cheeks. "We didn't mean to make you feel bad."

An exaggerated grunt came from Sam as he plopped himself down in the grass. Lucas followed suit, sitting down next to him. Rosie sighed. So much for being alone.

As Lucas stretched out his long legs, Rosie watched

him. The band T-shirt and faded jeans he wore were typical. His dirty Converse looked like they'd seen some muddy hikes through the woods. Lucas Beckett and his father, Roger, were the only two members of the pack who were not members of the Hart family. They'd joined the Hart pack when Lucas was six, after Roger challenged the Beckett pack alpha and lost.

At sixteen, Lucas towered over all the other boys his age. His thick brown hair fell in loose waves around his face. The locks looked soft, and Rosie often had to fight an urge to brush her hands through them. His sea-blue eyes were two beacons of bright light that peeked out from under his curtain of dark hair. On the rare occasion that something made him angry, the bright blue turned stormy and smoldered in a way that made her heart flutter.

Over the past year or so, the dynamic between Lucas and Rosie had changed. When they were pups, Sam, Lucas, and Rosie were inseparable. In human form, they played hide-and-seek and made mud pies. In wolf form, they played hunters and prey and chased squirrels. As they grew into their teenage years, the childish playfulness between Rosie and Lucas dissipated, leaving something different behind.

The youthful softness of Lucas's cheeks had given way to a chiseled jawline. His thin, gangly form turned long and lean with toned muscles and smooth, tanned skin. He was becoming a handsome man while she remained a red-haired, freckled, awkward kid. The carefree, playful ease of their relationship became somewhat strained as Rosie let her insecurities take over. That was her fault. Intimidated by his good looks, she was pulling away.

Rosie stared at the grass for a few seconds, trying to think of something to say.

"Do you guys want to go for a run tomorrow night?" she finally asked.

For werewolves, a run didn't mean a form of exercise. A run meant shedding their human form to run as wolves. Nothing beat the feel of wind rippling along their fur and hard ground vibrating beneath the pads of their big wolf paws. Whenever she felt a little lost, an evening run made the world feel right and whole again. The tedious affairs that plagued her as a human were forgotten as she returned to a more primal level of existence. The hunt became a thrilling need, and her existence became a stark contrast to who she was in human form. They weren't allowed to run alone, so Sam, Lucas, and Rosie often ran together.

Sam frowned and picked absently at the grass. "I can't. Dad wants me to go over pack stuff."

Rosie and Sam's father, Simon, was grooming Sam to be the pack alpha one day. To say Sam was reluctant was an understatement. At seventeen, he didn't take life seriously. Everything was fun and games, girls and sports. Simon had allowed his son to be a kid for too long, and now he was having trouble reining him in.

Rosie secretly rooted for her father to whip Sam into shape. The alternative to Sam as the future alpha was her father's creepy cousin, Amos. Every time Amos entered a room, a chill ran down her spine, and she tried her best to stay out of his way. The idea of him leading the pack sent a nervous jolt through her.

Luckily, that wasn't something she needed to worry about. Her dad would remain alpha until Sam was ready.

"What kind of 'pack stuff'?" Rosie asked in her best imitation of his glum tone.

"We're hosting a formal party here a week from Saturday, and before you ask"—his voice rose as she opened her mouth to interrupt—"you have to go."

"Crap," she breathed.

Simon worked hard to keep the peace with the two neighboring werewolf packs that roamed Northern Wisconsin in and around the Chequamegon-Nicolet National Forest. The Cramer pack occupied the northwestern part of the state, toward Minnesota. The Beckett pack roamed the northeast, toward Michigan, and the Hart pack lay between them.

The boundaries had been carefully negotiated and marked generations ago. The innate territorial werewolf trait defied logic and reason and made keeping the peace with other packs difficult. The three packs traditionally shared formal gatherings at least once a year to stay in touch and keep the peace.

Unfortunately, Rosie and Lucas had both turned sixteen within the last year, so Simon said they were old enough to start attending pack gatherings. Aside from the obvious—a formal dinner with a bunch of stuffy men would be beyond boring—Rosie dreaded attending any gathering with other wolf packs for the simple reason that she was female.

No other female werewolves existed. Rosie was the only one—the *only* one. Being the only girl in Hart House was awkward enough. She wasn't looking forward to being the only girl in a room full of werewolves from another pack too.

"Who are we meeting with?" Rosie asked warily.

"The Cramer pack," Sam said, making Rosie's heart sink. "William Cramer insisted we meet. He said he has business."

Tension had been high with the Cramer pack the last

two years since Bruce Cramer killed Jack Hart at the border between their territories.

Jack had been Rosie's favorite of her father's cousins. Simon always referred to him as an overgrown kid. He made up games and played with the pups when no one else would give them the time of day.

Bruce claimed Jack was in their territory and had been warned but Jack didn't back off. No one understood how it could've happened. The older pack members sometimes took vacations from human form and stayed in wolf form for days or weeks at a time, but they knew the borders. When Jack didn't return after three weeks, Simon had a private conference with the Cramer pack alpha then disappeared for a week. He came back with Jack's body.

According to Stuart, that wasn't the first time the Cramers had killed a member of the Hart pack. They were serious about their borders. One of the few packs left who turned up their noses at the Council's attempts to change the past. They kept up old werewolf traditions. Barbaric traditions.

"What do they want?" Rosie asked, not attempting to hide the disgust in her voice.

"They've had a few run-ins with a rogue," Sam said. "They want to know where he came from."

Rosie sighed and glanced toward the house. She guessed Simon was pacing the floor of his office as he usually did when pack business came up. The rogue couldn't have come from their pack, but William Cramer, the Cramer pack alpha, probably wanted to grill Simon anyway. If the rogue was causing trouble for the Cramer pack, William would no doubt want him gone. And if the rogue didn't go willingly, he would want him dead.

A shiver coursed through her body. The Cramers were brutal. How did they get away with acting so callously?

Thankfully, the Becketts didn't seem to be like the Cramers. Her Uncle Stuart told her stories about the Cramers that kept her up at night, but he made it sound like the Becketts weren't much different from the Harts. Were there other packs out there like the Cramers? God, she hoped not.

"Don't worry about it, Rosie," Sam said, nudging her bare foot with his sneaker. "I'm sure you'll blend in just fine."

"I'm not worried," she lied, kicking his foot away and rolling her eyes at his sarcasm. She tried to deflect and change the subject. "You guys are going to the party Friday night, right?"

Every year, someone from school hosted an end-of-the-year party. The high school had less than two hundred students, so most of the kids knew each other.

"I have a date with Heather Friday night, but I know you'll be there because it's at Ma-a-ason's house," Sam teased, accentuating Mason's name in a high-pitched singsong and batting his eyelashes at Rosie.

Hiding the crush she had on Mason Lewis was next to impossible with Sam and Lucas hovering over her everywhere she went. She growled at Sam as her cheeks grew hot. Truthfully, she really was looking forward to seeing Mason at the party. She'd been looking forward to it for weeks, in fact.

A weird noise came from Lucas, like he'd choked on his tongue, and when she glanced his way, he had a pinched expression she couldn't place. He looked away, and she wished for the millionth time that she could read his emotions. She hadn't been able to read him in years. Not since that day in the forest when they were kids. She could read every other person on the planet like an open book, but Lucas's emotions were hidden from her. It was simultaneously frustrating and alluring. While she would give anything to know what he was feeling, the break from the constant barrage of emotion was refreshing.

"I'll be there," Lucas said as he studied a nearby tree and shrugged nonchalantly. "Nothing better to do."

"Martha's coming." Sam's enhanced hearing picked up the sound of footsteps trudging through the grass before it caught Rosie's attention.

She tore her gaze away from Lucas's far-off stare. The waddling gait gave the old woman away.

Martha Morris was the only other female in the house. They fondly called her their den mother, and she was like family. She kept the house clean, cooked most of the meals, and raised Lucas, Sam, and Rosie. Most packs employed humans, usually women, for help around the house and with raising children. The human help stayed at the pack house and were bound to the pack for the rest of their lives, under threat of death. The Council had few laws they enforced, but keeping the werewolf world secret was first and foremost. Rosie tried not to think that anyone in their pack would kill Martha if she tried to leave, but that wasn't an issue. Martha never expressed a desire to leave.

Thick ankles and a limp made Martha look like a waddling duck. Her white hair was tucked up in a loose bun, and when she finally spotted them, she spoke with a very thick northern Wisconsin accent. "There you kids are." She yelled between panting breaths. Even a short walk winded the pudgy old woman. "I've been looking for you all over the place. It's suppertime!" She eyed Rosie and scowled. "Rose Hart, have you been sitting out here all afternoon?" Her scolding tone was like nails on a chalkboard. "Look at those muddy feet!"

"It's just a little dirt, Martha," Rosie grumbled as Lucas and Sam each reached out a hand to help her up from the ground.

"Don't you dare get sassy with me!" Martha wagged a finger in her direction as they started back across the lawn toward the house. "You're getting way too old to be climbing trees and running barefoot through the mud like a heathen."

"I'm sorry," Rosie mumbled though she didn't mean it.

She liked the feeling of earth between her toes. Her grandma, Clara, told her it was the best way to get in touch with nature—to experience it up close and personal. Rosie often got conflicting guidance from Clara and Martha.

As they neared the house, the smell of cooked venison permeated the air, and a low growl rumbled from Rosie's stomach.

"Hungry?" Lucas raised the corner of his mouth in a half smile.

Hearing, sight, and smell were enhanced for werewolves, especially while in wolf form. For the typical werewolf, those senses were still heightened in human form, though not as much. Rosie was the exception. Her senses were as enhanced as any other werewolf's while she was in wolf form, but they returned to normal when she was in human form. It was just another way she was different from everyone else.

"Always." Rosie grinned as she nudged him with a shoulder. "I could eat a horse."

"Rose Hart," Martha called over her shoulder. "Is that any way for a young lady to speak? For crying out loud, you'd think I raised you in a barn."

Sam and Lucas roared with laughter, and Sam gave her a playful shove. "Yeah, Rosie, be a lady."

She shoved him back then paused as a faint tingle worked its way up her spine. She slowed her pace and glanced back toward the woods as she touched her neck. She was being watched. She was sure of it. Goose bumps prickled her arms.

"Shake a leg, Rosie! Supper's getting cold."

Rosie snapped her head toward the sound of Martha's voice. She sighed, telling herself it was just an animal as she rushed to catch up to Martha and the boys.

TWO

LUCAS

"You're going down, Hart!"

"You wish! I got you, loser!" Sam held the game controller out in front of him and leaned to the right, as though that would make his kart move with him.

Lucas laughed as he hit Sam's kart with a red shell and soared past him to the finish line.

"Yes!" He jumped up from the couch and pointed at Sam. "You owe me five bucks!"

The high of winning was quickly squashed by the heavy weight of embarrassment when Rosie poked her head into the rec room.

"Are you guys betting on Mario Kart again?" she asked. "Dad will be pissed if he finds out."

Lucas's legs turned to mush, and he lowered himself onto the leather couch as she strolled to the armchair, where she sat, tucking her legs underneath herself. Red curls sprang in all directions from a haphazardly tied mess atop her head. Loose strands dangled down the sides of her face like coiled ribbons, and the color popped against her ivory skin. A pair of leggings decorated with cartoon animals hugged her legs, and an oversized University of Wisconsin hoodie swallowed up the top half of her body. Her hand was buried inside a box of Fruit Loops, fishing out pieces of cereal that she popped into her mouth. The crunch reverberated through the room, and her heart-shaped pink lips stretched into a smile as she watched the television screen.

"Dad won't find out if you don't tell him, doofus," Sam huffed. He fished a five-dollar bill out of his wallet and tossed it onto the polished, hand-carved coffee table.

Rosie stuck her tongue out at Sam. It was covered in little flecks of brightly colored cereal.

"Keep your money." Heat crept into Lucas's cheeks. "Rosie is right. We shouldn't be betting on this."

Sam stared at Lucas for a few seconds before shrugging and swiping his five from the table. "Suit yourself. Wanna go again?"

"Nah. I should probably study. You should too, Sam. You know your dad is going to be on your case. Might as well get started." Lucas flicked his gaze over to Rosie. "What about you, Rosie? You ready for your Spanish test?"

"Ugh, I need a break." She threw her head against the chair cushion. "I'm starting to hate that language. I used to think it was sexy."

Something in him jolted at her use of the word *sexy*, and he immediately wished he could speak Spanish. God, what was wrong with him? *Get a grip, Lucas.* He took a deep breath, and the smell of lavender incense traveled up his sensitive nose. Rosie always burned candles in her room. She said they kept the air positive, whatever that meant. It didn't matter. He believed anything that came out of her mouth. She could tell him she had the power to conjure unicorns, and he would believe it. He'd seen what she could do with his own eyes.

"Meh. I'm getting Cs. Good enough." Sam shrugged.

Rosie's brow crinkled in worry, and she frowned. "Sam, come on. You know Dad is going to be on you about it. He's going to yell at you, and it will all be for nothing because we all know you're smart enough to bring home better grades. Show him you're as smart as we all know you are."

"What does getting an A in literature prove? He'll just find something else to rag on me about." Sam rolled his eyes.

Rosie leaned forward and placed a hand on Sam's arm. "It proves you've got the discipline and intelligence to be a good alpha. That's all he wants. To know that you'll put your heart into it."

The tension in Sam's shoulders deflated visibly, and Sam sighed. Rosie's power to calm her brother was amazing. Lucas had seen her do it dozens of times.

"Fine." Sam tossed the controller onto the coffee table and stood.

Rosie smiled at him, and he touched her shoulder as he walked by, wandering out into the hallway toward the stairs.

As Rosie leaned back in the chair, she casually popped more cereal into her mouth as though the magic she'd just performed was no big deal. A few pieces of cereal missed her mouth and bounced down her leg. She brushed them off to the floor then sat up.

"Shoot. Martha will have my head." She slid down to the floor and started picking up the bits from the carpet.

Lucas watched her from his spot on the couch. "How did you do that?"

"What?" Rosie looked up at him, her brow creased in confusion.

"How did you get him to agree to go study? You know he was dead set against it."

Rosie picked herself up off the floor and plopped down on the couch beside Lucas. "His defiance is driven by fear and insecurity. He loves Dad. He doesn't want to disappoint him. I calmed him down. Took away the fear. For a little while, anyway. Unfortunately, it will come back. And when it does, he'll doubt himself again."

Lucas laughed. "You should just follow him around with your hand on his shoulder all the time."

Rosie smiled sadly. "I wish I could."

Lucas dropped his gaze to the floor and nodded. "Yeah."

A tinge of jealousy hit him. Rosie cared about Sam more than anyone else in the world, and though he admired their close bond, Lucas wished for more of her affection. He knew Rosie loved him—they had been best friends since they were six—but Lucas was pretty sure that's all he was to her. A friend.

He wanted more.

It was fair to say that Lucas had loved Rosie Hart since he was eight years old. The day she took his face in her hands and healed him—that was the day his heart became hers. Of course, it was only over the last couple of years when his teenage hormones started raging that his love started morphing into something different. It wasn't like he could act on it. They lived together. They were in the same pack. Her father was his alpha. She was his best friend. Besides that, she'd spent the last year practically ignoring him. They used to be so close. Now it sometimes seemed like they were strangers.

But then...

Sometimes, her eyes would soften when she looked at

him, and it would give him a surge of courage, and he would think maybe, just maybe, they could make it work. He'd started dropping hints to her about his feelings months ago, before she developed a crush on Mason Lewis. Of all the guys for her to fall for, it had to be the biggest jerk in the school. God, he hated Mason.

"You have a test tomorrow?" Rosie leaned back into the couch and propped one foot up in front of her. Her bare toes wiggled. The nails were painted black.

"Just calculus."

"Just calculus." Rosie rolled her eyes as she mimicked his nonchalant response. "You know, most people would be sweating over a calculus final. You were the same way with your other exams. I know you had the same lit final I had. I was up all night studying for that thing, and I know you were up late playing video games with Sammy. You still did better than I did."

Lucas shrugged. "I read a lot."

"I read a lot." Rosie raised her chin defiantly.

"Twitter doesn't count."

"Ha ha. Not all of us read boring books for fun." With a toe, Rosie nudged an old, faded paperback sitting on the coffee table, a copy of *The Odyssey*.

"Uh...Rosie, that was our assigned reading for literature class. You were supposed to be reading it too."

"I read it. It was boring." She smiled at him and gave him a playful shove. "Don't pretend it's your first time reading it."

She was right. He'd read it at least three other times.

"Oh...before I forget, I have a new playlist done if you want it," Lucas said.

Rosie seemed to like Lucas's taste in music, and she was always asking him for something to listen to through the noise-canceling headphones she often wore around other people. The rumor that flew around school was that she was on the spectrum, but Lucas knew they helped Rosie drown out the emotions that overwhelmed her. He'd been witness to some of the relentless teasing she endured for the way she withdrew from the world and hid behind the headphones, but she always seemed to let it roll off her back like it was nothing. She strolled through the halls, oblivious to the stares of the other kids.

"Yes, please!" Her eyes lit up in excitement.

He held out a hand. "Give me your phone."

After handing Lucas her phone, Rosie picked up the remote control to flip through the channels. She landed on an episode of a cheesy family sitcom, and an amused grin lit her face. Giggles floated through the air periodically as Lucas worked on downloading the playlist. Her laughter was like music, and he couldn't help the smile that crept across his face when he heard it.

"How can you watch that crap?" Lucas mumbled.

"Are you kidding? I love this show. Don't you ever wish you could have a life like that? Just...normal. A mom, a dad, kids. No hunting. No pack rules. No worrying about full moons. Just everyday stuff. Nothing weird."

A soft smile graced her lips as she spoke, but her sadness was palpable. Lucas knew it was hard for her. No werewolf had a normal life, but as the only female werewolf, Rosie's future was uncertain. Who knew what the Council would decide to do with her? Would they let her stay with the Harts? Would they force her to join another pack? Would they even continue to let her live? His stomach turned at the thought of them killing her, and he swallowed the lump that formed in his throat.

"All set," he said, handing the phone back to her. "It's all stuff you've heard before, I'm sure."

"Thank you."

As she touched his fingers, a tingle ran through his hand and raised the hair on his arm like static. Her eyes rounded, and her mouth formed an O before she bit her lip and looked away.

She stood up, and a whoosh of her scent hit him again. "Well…I guess I better get back to studying."

"Yeah," he said. "I guess I should too."

As he watched her walk out of the room, the tingle lingered in his arm.

THE EVENING SUN peeked through the treetops, casting shadows across the yard. Lucas sat on the patio and took it in. Summer was coming, and the days were getting longer, making the sunsets a soft sigh at the end of the day instead of the abrupt shutter of the early nights of winter. The sounds of the forest grew quiet as night descended.

"Lucas?" His father's voice from the doorway broke the peace of the evening.

Lucas closed his eyes. "Hey, Dad."

He listened to his father's soft footsteps as the man crossed the stone patio. He stopped next to Lucas and stood quietly for a few moments.

"It's a nice night," Roger said as he took a deep breath in through his nose.

"Yeah."

"Shouldn't you be studying?"

"I'm good. It's just calculus."

"Don't be cocky."

Lucas rolled his eyes and finally looked at his father. Roger grinned at him.

"So what's on your mind, kid?" Roger sat down in one of the empty patio chairs and leaned back.

"Nothing."

"Bull. You're thinking about a girl."

Traitorous heat filled his cheeks as he blushed, giving his father the answer he was looking for. He looked away, trying to hide his face. The last thing he wanted to do was talk about this with his dad.

"Okay, hint taken," Roger said with a laugh. The laugh died down, and his tone turned serious. "I heard from Shawn today."

"All quiet on the Beckett front?" Lucas asked, a nod to one of his favorite books. When silence met Lucas's question, he glanced at his father.

A pensive look was etched on Roger's face, and he glanced toward the house before he lowered his voice. "Marcus has been letting things slide. Shawn said he's drunk all the time. He lies around the house all day. Shawn is trying to keep things running, but he can't do it all. His talent is in the craft industry. He can't stay on top of the financial and political end of things."

Every pack had a business. The Hart pack had vacation and rental properties. The Cramer pack had logging. The Beckett pack had alcohol. The Beckett brewery was headquartered on the outskirts of Beckett Falls, a small town founded by and named for their family generations ago. The town was nestled in the northeast part of the state, not far from Nicolet National Forest. The rivers that cut through the rugged, wooded terrain created dozens of beautiful waterfalls, so it was a popular area for hikers. Many of the little town's residents worked at the brewery. The Bavarian-style architecture of the downtown area created a perfect backdrop for the town's version of Oktoberfest every fall, which drew visitors from all over.

Lucas would give his left arm to go there, but unfortunately, everything he knew of Beckett Falls and its brewery, he'd learned from his father and the internet. As a banished pack member, Roger couldn't step foot in Beckett territory, even in human form. Lucas wasn't technically banished, but it went without saying that he wasn't welcome.

Before he was banished, Roger had managed all financial matters for the pack and the brewery business. Roger's brother, Shawn, traveled the state, promoting their brand and staying current on trends in the industry. Their cousin, Travis, and their uncle, Christopher, kept things running in the brewery.

Roger leaned forward and rubbed his face. "I was afraid of this. I could see it coming a mile away. Marcus has always been a useless pile of crap. The only reason he's alpha is because his father wanted him to be. He's never shown the least bit of interest in what's best for the pack. All he cares about is himself." Roger swore under his breath before he looked at Lucas. "I didn't take the decision to challenge him lightly. I was afraid. I knew he would run the pack into the ground. I thought I could take him, but I underestimated him. He's a sloppy drunk, but he's strong. He wiped the floor with me."

Lucas looked away. Hearing his father admit his failures didn't sit well with him, but he knew Roger's strength was his mind, not his muscle. His tall, thin frame was almost gangly. Lucas had always been sure he would grow to look just like him, but he was pleasantly surprised to find himself filling out a little over the last couple of years. It helped that he liked to run, and sometimes he lifted weights with Sam and Sam's cousin Michael.

"Anyway, Shawn said he can't meet next Monday."

The first Monday of every month for as long as he could remember, Roger and Lucas had met with Shawn, Travis, and Christopher. Roger was determined to keep Lucas close to his family. Marcus knew nothing about the meetings, of course. If he did, he'd put an end to them.

Roger cleared his throat. "We're meeting with them on Friday instead—"

"Friday, I can't!" Lucas's heart leaped into his throat. "The end-of-the-year party is that night."

"We'll be home long before your party, Lucas. Don't worry."

Tension left his shoulders, and the knot in his stomach loosened. It was stupid. Why did he want to go to the party so badly? To watch Rosie fawn all over Mason?

Yeah. He wasn't looking forward to the party at all. But he would be there.

THREE
ROSIE

WHEN THE WORDS ON THE FLASHCARDS BLURRED together and she worried she might start conjugating verbs in her sleep, Rosie decided she'd done enough studying for her Spanish final. She stood up from her desk and stretched her arms above her head as she yawned. The candle on the shelf above her desk was reduced to a lump of wax with a wick in the middle. She silently reminded herself that she would need to ask her grandma to make her a new one as she leaned forward and blew out the flame. A thin trail of smoke floated up toward the ceiling, and she breathed in the calming smell of burnt sage.

Something made her turn her head toward her ficus, and she turned her lip out in a pout at its droopy appearance. Picking up the watering can from the floor, she stepped into the attached bathroom to fill it. After she gave the plant some water, she ran her fingers over its thick leaves and smiled in satisfaction as they perked under her touch. She moved around the room, giving attention to each of her plants, wetting their soil and sharing her energy to keep them lively.

As she returned her watering can to its spot on the floor, she noticed embedded dirt colored her short fingernails almost as black as the polish on her toenails. Her gaze trailed down to her dirty feet, and she blew out a huff of breath. She really needed a shower. Grabbing her robe along the way, she shuffled to the bathroom. As she passed her mirror, she noticed a slight pink tingeing her cheeks, the result of her afternoon in the sun. She stopped to study her face, sighing. Simon often talked about how beautiful her mother had been, and she hoped she would be just as beautiful one day. For now, she had a mess of curly red hair that tangled to her lower back. Long lashes framed her red-brown eyes, the one feature she appreciated about herself. Her skin was pale and freckled. Though she was barely five feet tall, her limbs were long and awkward—all elbows and knees, as her cousin Michael liked to say. She didn't have any real curves. Not like the other girls at school. Sometimes, she swore she looked like a scrawny twelve-year-old boy. No hips, a flat butt, and—worse yet—the tiny lumps on her chest barely filled an A cup.

After a hot shower, she dressed in an oversized T-shirt that hung to her knees, and she crawled into bed. Her phone flashed from the nightstand, prompting her to pick it up.

Fifteen unread messages—they had to be from Becca.

Rebecca Miller and Rosie had been best friends since the first day of kindergarten, when Becca coaxed Rosie through her first panic attack. The emotions had been too much. A room full of children, all terrified of their first day of school, had sent Rosie into a fit of hyperventilation. She'd covered her ears and squeezed her eyes shut, trying to block everything out. But then Becca took her hand and led her out of the room. She hugged Rosie close, shushing her and running a hand through her hair. They'd been best friends ever since.

They shared everything—well, almost everything. Rosie often felt guilty about keeping her wolf-and-witch heritage a secret, but it wasn't just her secret to keep. Her father had drilled into her from a very young age that the secret spanned hundreds of years and was much bigger than her guilty conscience. If their secret got out, it could be deadly to the pack.

Despite the guilt, keeping her friend in the dark had its advantages. With Becca, Rosie could be something that resembled a normal teenager. Though she held her heritage and everything that came with it close to her heart, she was also a teenage girl that just wanted to do teenage-girl things. She could always count on Becca for that.

Rosie sleepily scrolled through the messages, all droning on about Friday's party. It had been all Becca could talk about for the past two weeks. One message jumped off the screen at her, and she bolted upright in bed.

BECCA: *You're NEVER going to believe what I heard!!! Mason told his friends to make sure you're going to be at the party!!!!! Ahhhhh!!!*

Rosie wasn't the type to go fangirl on the captain of the football team, but Mason was different. Even though Rosie was growing up in a house full of men, she was terrified of talking to the boys at school. She didn't unless she had to.

During first semester, Rosie had been horrified when she was assigned Mason as her science partner. She dreaded class every day. Forced interaction with the most popular boy in school was right up there with medieval torture. It was a quiet, awkward partnership at first. He would say hi, and she would grunt a quiet hi in return before hiding beneath her headphones. One day, he noticed her scrolling through the latest blog posts on her favorite wildlife site and asked her about it. As it turned out, he was an avid wildlife enthusiast and frequented the same sites she did. At first, she was shy about it, but he was persistent. He would carry on about the blogs and articles he'd read, and she was pulled in. She couldn't resist talking to the only person she'd ever met who read the same things she did. It was so much better than scrolling and posting in the comments section. They spent the rest of the semester swapping blog recommendations and talking about the content. He was so passionate about the material, and when Rosie spoke, he watched her and listened so intently it made her feel...*heard*. Important. Seen.

Their conversations stopped at the end of the semester, but the crush she'd developed endured.

She quickly shot a text to Becca, asking if they could meet up Friday before the party. It would have to be at Becca's house. For obvious reasons, Simon didn't want people at Hart House for casual visits, so Becca had only been there a handful of times.

Rosie fell back onto her pillows and smiled up at the ceiling. Her mind raced. Did Mason like her? Did he want to date her? Could that really be possible? She began imaging long walks in the woods with Mason. Her summer was looking better...much better.

After about three hours of ping-ponging between staring at the ceiling and scrolling through random junk on her phone, Rosie finally gave up trying to fall asleep. With a tired grunt, she rolled out of bed and slipped off to the main kitchen. She ran a hand through her mess of curls and yawned as she padded barefoot to the refrigerator and peeked inside. She didn't know what she was looking for, but she would know it when she found it.

The only sound in the kitchen was the hum of the refrigerator, so when a voice came from behind her, she squealed and jumped, smacking her head on the fridge shelf.

"Hungry?"

Rosie spun around and found Lucas sitting silently at the kitchen table, a mug of what appeared to be hot chocolate in front of him. His lips spread into a "gotcha" smile.

Sighing, she rubbed her head and played into their earlier, predinner exchange.

"Always." She opened the freezer, pulled out a pint of ice cream, grabbed two spoons from the silverware drawer, and walked over to the table. Plopping down in the chair across from him, she wordlessly handed him a spoon and peeled the lid off the pint of mint chocolate chip.

"What are you doing sitting alone in the dark?" Rosie asked before ramming a spoonful of minty goodness into her mouth.

"Couldn't sleep," Lucas said simply as he dug his spoon into the ice cream.

"Don't tell me you're worried about your calculus final now," she teased.

Lucas was by far the smartest student in their class. He was the guy who knew all the trivial stuff and got As without breaking a sweat.

He cocked an eyebrow at her like she was crazy and shook his head.

Rosie rolled her eyes and took another bite. "What is it, then?"

"Just couldn't sleep, I guess. You?"

"Same." She shrugged. "And I guess I was kind of hungry."

"That's not surprising." He chuckled. "You barely ate at supper. You looked like you were off in la-la land."

Rosie paused mid-bite, holding the spoon in her mouth as she looked at him. If he noticed, that meant he'd been watching her at supper. He continued to stare, and she tried to identify the emotion on his face.

"Thinking about Ma-a-son?" He sing-songed Mason's name the same way Sam had earlier, but the teasing didn't sound lighthearted. It almost felt mean.

"No." She scowled, feeling a little hurt at his cross attitude. "Since when do you care, anyway?"

"I've always cared about you, Rosie. You know that."

Not really sure how to reply, Rosie concentrated on tracing her spoon around the outer lip of the ice cream, where it had melted. She knew he'd always cared about her as a pack member and a friend, but there was something really genuine in the way he said the words. She suddenly felt important to him.

God, how she wished she were more to him than the little misfit who hung out with he and Sam all these years.

Heat crept up her neck. He was witty, adorable Lucas, and she was just plain old Rosie.

"I know." She met his gaze briefly. A sudden thought took root in her mind, and her lips stretched into a coy smile. "You know the best cure for insomnia."

Lucas met her gaze and grinned, shaking his head slowly. "We'll get in trouble."

"I won't tell if you don't."

FOUR

ROSIE

Rosie and Lucas jumped up from the table, nearly knocking their chairs to the floor in their hurry to get outside. They weren't allowed to go out for a run without permission from one of the older wolves, but a run was just what Rosie needed. She wanted to get school and the rest of the human world out of her head for a little bit. Plus, a run always made her tired, which was the perfect remedy for insomnia.

When werewolves shifted, it wasn't like in the movies. It was almost instantaneous rather than painful or slow. After disrobing, they usually took a running start, leapt, and changed in midair. Unfortunately, Sam, Lucas, and the rest of the pack had grown accustomed to seeing Rosie naked. It was inevitable when shifting into and out of wolf form. She tried to be discreet, but it was nearly impossible.

After they shifted, Lucas and Rosie raced toward the forest. She could feel him beside her as she wove through the trees. Twigs and pine needles crunched under her paws. The trees towered overhead, and above the treetops, stars were sprinkled over the inky blackness of the night sky.

Branches and leaves whipped at her face as she sprinted through thick foliage. Lucas's feet pounded against the earth a few steps behind, and he nipped at her tail as he shot ahead.

As a werewolf, Rosie felt her senses come alive. She could hear mice running through the brush and smell the flowers from the yard back at the house even though they'd already run almost a mile. A raccoon climbed a tree over a hundred yards away, yet she could see its fur blowing in the wind. She relished the feeling.

"We shouldn't go too far," Lucas said as he slowed down.

He broke left before he reached a clearing with a small pond, and she soared past, diving in. Water splashed around her as she bounced up and down, trying to catch droplets in her mouth. Muddy pond scum coated her fur, but she didn't care. She paused, letting her tongue hang out one side of her mouth as she panted happily.

The sound of Lucas's paws hitting the forest floor stopped, and he turned back toward her. She was about to call out to him when she caught a whiff of something on the breeze. It smelled like tobacco and aftershave and—

"Rosie, look out!"

Lucas's warning came a second too late. The gun blasted, and the bullet pierced the water inches away from her.

"Run, Rosie!" he screamed.

She jumped from the water and took off in the direction of the house. Another gunshot echoed through the night, and the brush under her feet exploded as the bullet pierced the earth.

Hunters shouldn't have been there. The Harts owned thousands of acres of private land, and the local hunters knew her father didn't tolerate trespassers. Occasionally, a hunter from down south would wander through, not realizing they were on private land. Simon usually ran them off himself. Sometimes, he got the local sheriff involved. Regardless, a hunter out in the middle of the night was beyond strange, especially since it wasn't hunting season.

"Run! Run home!" Lucas yelled as he turned toward the hunter.

"Lucas!" Rosie watched in horror as Lucas ran straight toward the danger. He zigzagged, attempting to draw the hunter's attention.

"Just go, Rosie!" he yelled.

Another gunshot whizzed past her ear, hitting the tree in front of her, and she scrambled toward the house. Panic gripped her, and she pumped her legs as fast as they would go.

Pop!

A startled whimper tore from her throat as a bullet pierced the ground in front of her. She slid to a halt and looked back. Lucas was nowhere to be seen.

"Lucas!" Her telepathic scream was met with silence.

Pop! Pop!

She cried out in pain and surprise as she felt a burn on her hindquarters.

"Rosie!" Lucas's panicked telepathic voice sounded far away.

Vicious growling mixed with another round of gunfire, followed by the sound of an ATV engine. Terrified, she ran again. The house appeared in the distance, and she pushed her legs as hard as she could, fear and worry making her stomach clench. Her pace slowed as she approached the yard, and she concentrated, listening for Lucas. When she finally heard his paws thudding near the house, she released a long sigh of relief. The roar of the ATV grew faint.

A soft whine escaped her throat as she sat on the ground, the pain in her leg making itself known. She licked at the wound, trying to assess the damage.

"Rosie." Lucas's telepathic voice was punctuated by the sound of heavy wolf panting as he rushed to her side. With a paw, he gently pushed her head away from the wound and began licking it.

"It's just a scratch," she said after shifting back to human form. Her hands roamed down her thigh to the spot above her knee where the bullet had hit.

Lucas licked a few more times then shifted to human form. He leaned in, inspecting and poking at the wound with his fingers.

"Ouch! Stop that!"

Lucas snapped his head up to look at her face and dropped his hands from her leg. "Sorry, I didn't mean to hurt you."

"You didn't hurt me," she hissed through her teeth. "A bullet did."

Lucas seemed to pale slightly more each time he glanced down at the wound, and his brow furrowed in anger as his blue eyes turned cold. There he went, looking all smoldering and gorgeous again. Rosie shyly covered her naked chest.

"We need to tell Simon," he said.

"Are you nuts?" she asked. "That's the last thing we need to do!"

"Rosie—"

"No!" she insisted. "Do you have any idea how angry he'll be?"

"Yeah, but this is dangerous."

She knew he was right, but if her dad found out, she'd probably be grounded. And there would go Friday's party.

"I don't think you get it," Lucas said. "He was *aiming* for you."

"Um, yeah, I caught on to that when he shot me," she said angrily. "I'm not stupid."

"No, Rosie," he said. "He was after *you*. I tried to lead him away from you, but he ignored me. He wanted you."

That was a piece of news she wasn't expecting, and it knocked her backward like a punch to the gut. She leaned on an arm, attempting to hide her fear.

"Maybe he liked my red fur and wanted my pelt." Her stomach churned in disgust as she said the words, but she tried to make light of it. "I guess he has a thing for redheads."

"This isn't funny, Rosie!" His smoldering blue eyes turned icy. She knew his anger was directed at the hunter, but she still flinched at his tone. "Somewhere out there, a hunter is looking for you. And he's out hunting in the middle of the night on your father's land. This isn't your typical, everyday hunter. Your dad has to know about this."

"I'm sorry," Rosie said. "I know, I know."

His shoulders sagged in relief.

"But can we wait until after Friday night?" she asked hopefully. "If we tell him now, he won't let me go to the party. Please, Lucas?"

Lucas cocked his head as he pinned Rosie with a disbelieving stare. He huffed out a breath. "Fine," he said, seething. "We'll wait. Wouldn't want you to miss the party."

He stood up and stomped back toward the house, his shoulders tense. Rosie watched him go and felt equal parts guilty and confused. She knew she'd hit a nerve, but she wasn't sure why.

He stopped suddenly and turned to her. "Well?" he said impatiently. "Are you coming?"

Rosie blinked at him, confused.

"Rosie, I'm not leaving you out here alone with a hunter on the loose."

She pushed herself up from the ground, wincing at the stab of pain in her thigh, and limped along behind him. Her leg would be sore for a few days, but things could have been worse...*much* worse.

FIVE

ROSIE

Rough pounding on the door ripped Rosie from a deep sleep.

"Rosie!" her father bellowed. "Get up! Breakfast in twenty minutes."

She bolted upright, cast a quick glance at her bedside clock, and groaned when she realized she'd slept through her alarm. She stretched, ready to jump out of bed, but a stabbing pain in her leg stopped her. Memories of the night before crashed down on her, and she tore her covers back to look. The wound was still there, a nasty red streak marring her thigh, surrounded by a dark, ugly bruise.

She carefully scooted out of bed, mumbling, "Ow, ow, ow," under her breath as she shuffled her bare feet across the carpet to the bathroom. She grabbed her toothbrush and glanced in the mirror, and her jaw dropped when she saw her reflection. Sticks and debris were tangled in her messy hair, and mud caked her face and arms.

"Crap," she mumbled, remembering her jaunt through the muddy pond.

Rosie quickly threw off her nightshirt and jumped in

the shower. She spent the next ten minutes washing mud off her arms and combing leaves out of her hair. After she was satisfied all evidence of the previous night's excursion was gone, she stepped out of the shower and dried off. She twisted her hair up into a loose bun and rushed to the closet to pick out some clothes.

After settling on a pair of capri-length jeans, to cover her wound, and a blue T-shirt, she spritzed some perfume on her leg. No blood oozed from the wound, but the bullet had pierced the skin, and her lupine family members could smell fresh blood from something as small as a needle prick.

She grabbed her backpack from the floor and shoved her books inside. With a grunt, she dragged the overstuffed bag behind her as she limped down the stairs, dropping it on the floor at the bottom. She steadied her gait to try to hide the limp as she entered the dining room. Breakfast had already started, and she caught Lucas's eye as she took a seat next to her cousin Daniel.

"Nice of you to join us," her father said. "Up late studying?"

Rosie took a large bite of toast and nodded, avoiding his stare.

"You missed out on some conversation," he said. "I was just saying that no one is to go out running for the next few nights."

She sucked in her breath sharply, inhaling bread-crumbs that sent her into a coughing fit.

"What?" Her voice rasped like an old lady's, and she glanced toward Lucas before she could catch herself. Had he told?

He stared at his plate, avoiding her.

"I heard gunshots last night." Simon raised an eyebrow at her as she continued patting at her chest, trying not to cough. "I'll go out and see what I can find today. If we have a hunter around here, I want everyone on two legs until he's gone. There's been a rise in cases of livestock killing, and some of the local hunters are gunning for wolves. The state is considering an off-season hunt. Some of the village board members have been after me to allow hunting on my land. The complaints are getting loud. I've refused their requests, of course, but that doesn't mean we won't have some trigger-happy trespassers to contend with."

That would explain the hunter from last night. The Harts owned miles of land that surrounded the town, and of course, Simon had a zero-tolerance policy on trespassers. The land had been procured by the Hart family over the course of several generations, growing the area where they could roam freely in wolf form.

Rosie studied the eggs on her plate and wondered if she should tell her father about the night before. If she didn't, she would be caught in a lie. If she did, she would be grounded before the party.

"Rosie," Simon snapped. "Are you listening to me?"

"Yes, sir," she said quickly. "No running. Got it."

Guilt gnawed at her as Lucas played with his food. She was dragging him into her lie. He looked up from his plate and met her eyes, shrugging with a smile as though forgiving her, and she wondered if she was the only one at the table with heightened empathy.

A stab of pain from her wounded leg caused her to flinch, and her knee banged into Daniel's. She shot him a quick apologetic smile as he glanced her way, his eyes questioning. Daniel, the oldest of Jack's two sons, had a quiet, easygoing spirit. She held a soft spot for him because they shared some of the responsibility of keeping the estate beautiful. Daniel did all the heavy lifting. He took care of the mowing, the hedge trimming, the pruning, and the weeding. Rosie's job was to help make everything grow, and she was good at it. Others would say she had a green thumb, but it was more of an innate gift—literally. It was part of her "freaky witch magic" as Sam would say. Watching the flowers bloom with a touch of her fingers was empowering and beautiful. Daniel had always been fascinated, and sharing the gift with someone who appreciated it so deeply was refreshing.

Jack's other son, Michael, couldn't be more different from Daniel. Michael's jack-of-all-trades type of talent made him handy around the house, and he took care of a lot of the household maintenance. His stocky, muscular build was fueled by a steady diet of venison and beer. Like Jack, Michael was truly a child at heart, but like a child, he had a short temper. He was hotheaded, and he'd carried a hatred for the Cramer pack since his father's death. For that reason, Simon tended to keep him away from all pack business relating to the Cramers. Rosie guessed that her father would send him away the night of the Cramers' visit.

Rosie picked mindlessly at her food, half-heartedly listening to Roger drone on about financial matters with Simon. When Roger and Lucas had joined the pack and moved into Hart House, Roger took over the role of accountant, and Simon was thankful for his expertise. Roger *looked* like an accountant. He had blue eyes like Lucas and a tall, rail-thin build. Rosie could feel a strong sense of loss and loneliness from him. He talked fondly about his pack and tried to keep memories of it alive for his son. Sometimes, she felt like they were just waiting at Hart House until going back was safe. She hoped not because the thought of losing Lucas—or any pack member—scared her.

"So..." Michael spoke up in his booming voice, cutting

off the financial drivel. His tone said he was in a ribbing mood, making her stomach flip nervously when his stare zeroed in on her. "What's this I hear about our little Rosie having a little crush? What's his name?"

A howl of laughter and a catcall whistle sounded from across the table, and Rosie shot a dirty look at Sam before covering her face with her hands.

"Mason Lewis," Sam supplied.

"As in Paul Lewis?" Simon asked.

The teasing smirk disappeared from Sam's face as he glanced toward his father. "Yeah, Paul Lewis is Mason's dad."

Simon sighed and looked at Rosie. "Paul Lewis has been a thorn in my side for years. He owns a patch of hunting land just south of our property line, and he's always trying to get away with crossing onto our land. If Mason is anything like his father, I don't want him anywhere near you, Rosie."

A jolt of anger ran through her, but she tried her best to school her expression. "I don't think he's anything like his father, Dad. He's always been nice to me."

"I still want you to stay away from him."

Rosie's heart sank. She slid down in her seat and crossed her arms, the sting in her sinuses telling her tears were coming. She clenched her teeth to try to quell them.

Simon sighed and ran a hand over his face. "I just don't want you near that kind of danger. Paul Lewis is ruthless. He sets inhumane traps and hunts illegally—"

"So, is he dreamy?" Michael propped his head on his hands and blinked at her.

"Seriously?" she mumbled. Heat rushed up her face and reached her ears, but she was thankful for her cousin's interference. No one else would dare interrupt Simon, but

Michael had such charm, her father just let out an annoyed huff of breath and a dismissive wave of his hand.

"Aw, we love you, Rosie," Daniel said with a smile.

Rosie returned his smile shyly before a strong negative energy wiped it from her lips. She glanced across the table to find Amos staring at her like a piece of dirt on the bottom of his shoe. Apparently, he didn't find the news of her crush so amusing. Rosie was used to his disapproving stare. An annoyed frown was permanently etched on his clean-shaven face. His sharp, pressed clothes were never rumpled. He didn't talk much, but when he did, he always seemed to be arguing or voicing disapproval.

She wiggled in her chair uncomfortably, trying to think of a way to change the subject. "So, Dad," she said, turning toward her father. "The Cramer visit—"

"You and Lucas will be there," he said. He knew Rosie well enough to know she would try to weasel out of it. "Formal attire. Martha will help you get something to wear."

She groaned and slumped in her chair again. Sam and Lucas shot sympathetic looks her way. Her father seemed to know her pain as well. A muscle twitched in his strong jaw, and his brow furrowed as his tanned face pinched in a frown. She didn't think he was particularly fond of letting the other packs near her, but he didn't have much choice.

"Just..." He sighed as he ran a hand through his short brown hair. Then he pinned her with a stare. Though they all shared the same eye color, Simon's were more expressive than most. Windows to his soul. "Just keep quiet and out of the way. Stay close to one of the pack at all times. If one of the Cramers approaches you—"

"I'll put a dent in his face," Michael finished.

"You won't be there, Michael," Simon said impatiently. "I have business for you in Hanks Hollow."

Looking unsurprised, Michael didn't hide his angry scowl. "Fine," he grumbled.

"You can stick close to me, Rosie," Daniel said. "None of them want to talk to me. They'll stay away."

Rosie smiled at Daniel. He was right. As one of Jack's sons, Daniel would be avoided by the Cramers. They wouldn't want to chance a fight outside their own territory.

"It is tradition for all members of a pack to be present," Stuart said.

When he spoke, everyone listened. Biologically, Stuart was grandfather to only Daniel and Michael, but they all thought of him as their grandpa. He knew everything about pack history and maintained a library of old journals from previous generations. His quiet voice rarely spoke up except to regale the pack with stories of his youth or interesting tidbits about pack history. He and Rosie used to have story time every night. She would sit on his lap, and he would read to her from his journals. She held their relationship close to her heart. Stuart rarely spoke to anyone else.

"Except for the pups, of course," he continued. "Having all members of a pack present is respectful."

"Agreed," Simon said patiently. "But I don't think the Cramers will take offense to Michael's absence."

Stuart raised an eyebrow but didn't say anything more. Rosie felt some frustration from him and wondered if he wanted Michael present at the Cramer visit because he knew Michael wouldn't be able to resist the urge to rip out Bruce Cramer's throat. He scrunched his face in an irritated scowl, but when he flicked his gaze toward Rosie, he winked before turning his attention back to his plate.

Stuart seemed like he'd been aging faster since Jack's

death. His gray hair turned whiter by the day, and age spots littered his arms. His hands showed a slight tremor, and his gait had slowed to a sloth's pace. Stuart's age and Daniel's and Michael's hatred for the Cramers made the three of them unsuitable as future alphas.

"What kind of business do you have for me in Hanks Hollow?" Michael asked.

Simon cleared his throat. "I need you to clean the gutters in a few of the properties around the lake. And I need you to get your passport. You're going to Canada in a few weeks."

Silence filled the room as Michael glanced at Simon. Everyone knew why Michael was going to Canada. The anger Rosie felt from Amos put a bad taste in her mouth. She glanced his way and flinched at the way he glowered at her father.

"I received the call from the Legacy Agency yesterday. They have a surrogate lined up. They just need your...er... deposit." As the silence lingered in the room, Simon sighed. "I know you're not keen on being a father, Michael, but we need to grow our pack. We need to think about our next generation."

A bang rattled the silverware on the table and made everyone jump. All eyes turned to Amos. He was sitting in his chair, his face red, his hand on the table where he'd slammed it down. "This is preposterous. This is what our pack has been reduced to?"

A feral growl came from Rosie's father as he stared at his cousin. His eyes glowed yellow, and his lip curled. "Watch yourself, Amos."

Amos averted his stare, dipping his head in submission. "Forgive me, Simon. It's just...Why pay a surrogate agency to birth our own offspring?"

"You know why. We've come a long way. Times have changed. We don't hunt and abuse women the way our ancestors did. Not in this pack."

"So our future is a bunch of test tube babies? Come on! Are we just going to erase the traditions passed down for hundreds of years?"

Simon stood so abruptly that his chair tumbled backward to the floor, the crash reverberating loudly through the room. "When the traditions call for murdering innocent women, then yes!"

"Innocent women? There's no such thing as an innocent woman."

"Enough!"

Rosie shrank in her chair. It wasn't very often that a werewolf shifted involuntarily, but enough anger could push a change. Simon shook where he stood, and Rosie was afraid he would shift right on top of the breakfast table.

Amos kept his gaze down as he folded his napkin and set it carefully on the table. "Please excuse me."

The screech of the chair echoed in the silent room as Amos stood from the table. He nodded toward Simon, turned on his heel, and quickly made his way out of the room. It wasn't the first time a scenario like this had played out. Amos always stopped just shy of sending Simon over the edge. Her father had the patience of a saint.

The air was thick with apprehension as all eyes turned to Simon. Several moments passed before he silently picked up his chair, set it upright, sat down, and spoke as though nothing had happened.

"So how are finals going?" he asked. He didn't address anyone directly, but the question was obviously aimed at Sam.

Rosie decided to save her brother and jump in. "Almost

done," she said giddily, trying to lighten the mood. "I have a Spanish final today, and then I can kiss sophomore year goodbye."

"I have a calculus final today," Lucas said, his voice a little shaky. "Otherwise, I'm all done too."

Simon smiled tightly as he focused his attention on Sam.

"Um," Sam mumbled, "I have two left."

"Which two?" Simon asked.

"American government and English literature," Sam said quietly.

"Ahhh," Simon said softly. "The two you're getting Cs in. Let's hope those finals bring your grades up."

"Yeah." Sam stared at his plate.

"Sam," Simon started, "it's not just the grades. I need you to learn. These are skills you'll need one day."

"Yeah," Sam said impatiently, dropping his fork onto his plate and rolling his eyes to the ceiling. "I get it."

"Watch it," Simon snapped.

"Yes, sir." Sam straightened in his chair. He shot a quick glance at Rosie, and she gave him a reassuring smile.

"Dad," Rosie said quickly. "Can I stay out past curfew Friday night?"

She already knew the answer, but she had to ask anyway. Plus, the question drew the conversation away from Sam's academics.

"Absolutely not," he said, still staring at Sam. "And I trust you will not be engaging in any drinking or other illegal activity at this *party*." He shifted his stare to Rosie.

She shrank into her chair. "Yes, sir."

"All right," Sam said, standing up. "My first final is at eight, so we gotta go."

Rosie shoveled more eggs into her mouth like a toddler

about to have her plate taken away, grabbed three more pieces of toast for the road, then stood from the table and followed Sam and Lucas out of the dining room. She picked up her overstuffed backpack, which she'd left at the bottom of the stairs, swinging it over one shoulder as she shoved half a piece of toast into her mouth and followed the boys outside.

The three of them shared a black Ford Explorer. Sam had argued for a more expensive vehicle, but their father insisted this would fit in better with the other cars in the high school parking lot. He gave in a little to Sam's pleas and got them a higher trim level, so the SUV came with all the bells and whistles that made it fun. They were supposed to take turns, but Sam never let Lucas or Rosie drive.

After crawling into the back seat, Rosie took out her Spanish flashcards. She studied the words while she munched on her toast, spilling crumbs all over the black leather seat.

Hart House was a few miles outside Hanks Hollow, a picturesque tourist town in the middle of northern Wisconsin. Tucked into a hollow of bluffs and surrounded by miles of forest, it was a remote little slice of heaven straight off the cover of a greeting card. The southern edge of town bordered Mingan Lake, where cottages and resorts lined the beaches and boasted beautiful sunset views. The boardwalk had a variety of small shops and bars and was perfect for an evening stroll. A picture-perfect main street had elaborately decorated storefronts where clothing, fudge, candles, and other souvenirs were sold. Though the tourist season peaked in summer, the town also drew a crowd late in the year when the streets were festively decked out for fall and the Christmas season.

As the oldest family in the area, the Harts owned most

of the property along the lake, in addition to most of the forest surrounding the town. The family gave back to the community by pouring money into the town and schools. It was one of the ways Simon said he maintained a good relationship with the humans. A good relationship meant fewer prying, suspicious eyes.

Rosie looked forward to summer and hoped to be able to spend some time in town. Most of the beaches had soft, warm sand, perfect for lying out in the sun. Boating and tubing were common pastimes on the lake, and almost every weekend, people gathered in the park for music, campfires, and food.

Sam pulled the SUV into the school parking lot. The three climbed out, and Rosie winced when she heard Jared Kent scream, "Freak!" She grabbed Sam's sleeve as he clenched his fists and took a step in Jared's direction.

"Leave it, Sam." She didn't let go of his sleeve until he turned toward her, his brow creased in concern. "It's not worth it. If you say something, it will only make it worse."

Sam shook his head. "I don't know why you don't stand up for yourself."

Rosie shrugged. "I don't care," she lied. "Don't worry about it, Sammy. Focus on your finals. You're going to do great."

The corner of Sam's mouth quirked up in a half grin. Lucas stood behind him, silently watching Rosie.

"I'll see you guys this afternoon." Rosie gave them a little wave before she turned away and strolled across the parking lot.

Though the morning was cool, the smell of summer was in the air. She had time to kill before her own final, so she found a spot on the grassy terrace that sprawled behind the school. After sitting on the grass, she pulled her backpack into her lap and fished her flash cards out of the front pocket. She stared at them, reciting the terms in her head and committing them to memory. A mixture of energies floated in the breeze, and her attention strayed from studying to watching her classmates mill around.

A spike of nervousness from a few feet away drew her gaze to a girl sitting on a blanket with an English textbook. Her face was scrunched in concentration as she studied the material closely. A loud whoop behind her caught her attention as a boy walked across the grass. Relief emanated from him as he strolled toward the parking lot, and she guessed he'd just finished his last final for the year. She closed her eyes and soaked in the light, happy energy he projected.

Opening herself up to the energy of the people around her in a crowded space—like taking a deep breath through her nose—was always a risk. It was usually fine, but it could be overwhelming if something rotten was in the air. When she was young and hadn't learned control, she had a number of panic attacks when the emotions got too strong. That was when kids started calling her a freak. The panic attacks stopped when she got older and learned to control her empathy, but the freak label stuck.

Most of the time, Rosie tried to tune out the people around her. She wore noise-canceling headphones to drown everything out. Teenage angst was always heavy in the air at school, and she usually just didn't want to deal with it.

The ringing of the bell signaled the end of first period, and Rosie gathered up her things. She maneuvered her way through the crowded hallway toward her classroom and barely made it through the door before the next bell rang. After taking a seat toward the back of the room, she buried her face in her hands and tried to close herself off from her classmates' test jitters. She shook off a shiver and reached for her headphones, fastening them over her head and ignoring the stares from the kids around her.

She closed her eyes and took a deep breath in through her nose. Letting the breath out slowly through her mouth, she felt the tension leaving her body. She took several more deep breaths and let herself get lost in the music thumping against her ears. As she opened her eyes again, she caught the disapproving stare of Mrs. Gordon, her teacher. Slowly, she pulled the headphones off and stuffed them into her backpack.

Her history of panic attacks had earned her several trips to the doctor as a child, and she'd been diagnosed with some form of anxiety. Her father knew the true reason behind the attacks and refused the doctor's recommended medications, but her diagnosis came with special accommodations at school. She was allowed the use of her headphones to calm herself. If she wanted, she could push back at her teacher and insist on keeping the headphones on, but it was so much easier not to argue. A few minutes behind the safety of the headphones was usually enough to calm her.

The late night of studying paid off, and she sailed smoothly through the exam. After checking and double-checking her answers, she walked her answer sheet to the front of the classroom. She placed it at the top of the pile and met Mrs. Gordon's eyes as she pulled her headphones back out of her backpack and placed them back on her ears. The teacher rolled her eyes and shook her head as she went back to grading papers. Rosie could feel the woman's disgust, and a knot of frustration coiled in her stomach.

Students weren't the only ones who thought of her as a freak.

Adjusting her backpack on one shoulder, Rosie walked out of the classroom and down the hall. Sophomore year was officially done, and the relief of finishing the year made it easier to let Mrs. Gordon's feelings roll off her back.

As she stopped at her locker, she wondered briefly how Sam was doing on his finals. She entered the combination on her lock and sighed as she pulled the door open. Hoping she had enough room in her backpack for all the crap she'd accumulated over the year, she started clearing things out—her gym clothes, her extra sweatshirts, her magazines, her books.

Squatting, she absently threw pencils, pens, and notebooks into her bag. As she grabbed a pile of books from the floor, her locker door slid shut, and she looked up, startled. Mason Lewis stared down at her, and that familiar flutter was back in Rosie's stomach. Mason's smile reached his bright-blue eyes, and her stomach clenched. What was it about him?

Rosie pushed her headphones off the top of her head, letting them slide down to her shoulders, where they rested around her neck.

He leaned against her locker and stared down at her. It was the way he looked at her—like he cared, like she was a person and not just the weird girl everyone ignored.

"Hi, Rose."

Rosie needed a moment to shake off her shock. He was talking to her. They hadn't really spoken since the end of last semester.

"Um. H-hi." She flinched at her stammering as she stood up. Why was she so awkward?

"Did you catch yesterday's post on the Wildlife Now site?"

Had she? Of course she had. It was about the wolf population in Yellowstone National Park. She could've said a million things about it.

All she managed was another stammer. "Y-yeah."

"Of course you did," Mason laughed and touched her elbow, making her breath catch in her throat as he continued. "What did you think?"

Bobbing her head like an idiot, she finally managed to blurt out a sentence. "It was really good."

"It was." He smiled again, and butterflies fluttered in her stomach. "I never would have thought reintroducing wolves to the wild could make such a huge difference." He paused. "I like talking to you. You aren't like other girls. You're different."

Heat rushed to Rosie's cheeks again, and she averted her gaze, zeroing in on the floor tiles as her heart sank. *Different.*

"So, the party Friday," he said smoothly. "I'm looking forward to it. My parents let me buy a keg."

"Oh?" She wasn't sure what else to say to that. Cool? Neat?

With great effort, she tore her gaze away from the floor and looked at him. His eyes were wandering up and down her body, and he licked his lips. Something was cringy about the way he did that, and she tensed, pulling her books up to cover her chest. He seemed to realize she'd noticed him looking and snapped his gaze back up to her face.

"You're going to be there, right?" he asked. The hope in his expression made Rosie forget the creepy vibe she'd gotten a moment ago, and she turned to mush all over again. It was his eyes. They made her melt. So sincere. So warm.

"Um. I think...I mean...yeah." Rosie sighed at her stutter. "I was planning on it."

Mason smiled. "I'll see you there."

He held her gaze as he took a few steps backward into the crowd of students trailing down the hallway. Rosie tried to break her stare as he turned on his heel and walked away, but she was entranced. She didn't care what her father said. She had no intention of staying away from Mason Lewis.

Out of nowhere, Becca jumped in front of Rosie, breaking her from her trance. Becca was taller than Rosie and fuller in all the right areas. Her smooth, tanned skin glowed under a full head of beautiful blond hair.

"Oh. My. God!" she squealed. "What did he say?"

"He asked if I'm going to the party Friday," Rosie said, a grin tugging at her lips.

Becca grabbed Rosie's upper arm and shook it, unable to contain her excitement. "Oh my God. What are you going to wear? You have to let me do your makeup."

As Rosie smiled at her, she caught sight of Lucas. He was talking to a couple of his friends across the hall, and he glanced her way. She wondered if he'd been there when she was talking to Mason.

For some reason, she really hoped he hadn't.

SIX
ROSIE

The rest of Rosie's day was spent on the terrace, watching her classmates sign yearbooks and say goodbye to each other. She smiled to herself as Becca did her social butterfly thing, dancing from one crowd of friends to another, chatting easily with each clique, a happy smile decorating her beautiful face. She glanced toward Rosie and waved. Rosie gave a small wave in return but stayed put. Sometimes, Rosie wondered why they were friends. They were nothing alike. Becca was always trying to get Rosie out of her shell, but Rosie was determined to stay in the shadows, where she was safe. The smile disappeared from Rosie's face. People like Mason didn't notice girls like Rosie. She wondered if Becca had talked her up to Mason. Her heart thumped wildly, and heat rushed to her cheeks. God, she really hoped not.

Sighing, she waved goodbye to Becca as she gathered her things and made her way to the parking lot to meet Sam and Lucas at the SUV. As she walked across the half-empty lot, she watched as Sam leaned against the driver's side door, talking to Lucas. She concentrated on trying to read

Sam's energy as she approached. She couldn't feel any strong emotions from him, so she watched his face closely, trying to gauge his expression. He gave her a half smile as if he knew she was trying to read him.

"I might have pulled my grades up to Bs." His anxiety ramped up as he spoke. "Maybe."

"Bs are good," she said with a reassuring smile. She touched his arm and pushed a calming energy through her fingers, and he relaxed.

He grinned. "Thanks, Rosie."

Lucas was quiet as the three of them climbed into the SUV.

Rosie nudged his shoulder. "Did your calculus final go okay, Lucas?"

"Of course it did," he said with a grin. "How about your Spanish final?"

"It was fine." She gave a half shrug.

He looked away, and Rosie sat back in her seat then pulled her headphones and a book out of her backpack. As Sam drove them home, she stared at the blur of trees as they raced by, bobbing her head slightly to the mix Lucas had compiled for her. She stole a few glances at him as she tried to get interested in the book that lay open in her lap. He stared silently out the window the entire ride home, and Rosie wondered what he was thinking.

A small indentation in the trees ahead marked the entrance to the Hart estate, and Sam pressed the button on the remote control that opened the large iron gate at the base of the driveway. He steered the SUV to the enormous garage and parked inside. Rosie climbed out and was met with an off-key tune hollered from outside.

She and the boys followed the sound to the shed behind the garage, where Michael was processing some deer meat.

Wearing a bloodstained apron, he sang loudly, raising his arms in the air and flashing rock-and-roll hand signals.

"Schoo-ool's out for summer!" He stuck his tongue out and mimicked a guitar solo.

Sam and Lucas chimed in, and Rosie let out a bark of laughter.

"Rosie!"

She turned as Daniel appeared from the backyard, propping a shovel on his shoulder as he strolled toward her. His black hair was tousled and wet with sweat, and dirt smeared his face and white shirt. Daniel was tall with an athletic build. A majority of his workday was spent outside, so he had a golden tan that stayed with him even through the winter. If he could pry himself away from the gardens every once in a while, he would have hordes of girls chasing him.

"The roses are looking beautiful. You've been paying some attention to them, I see."

"I didn't need to do much," Rosie said honestly. "They're always pruned, and I've yet to see a weed bothering them. You keep them very happy. The peonies were a little upset, but I don't think that's your fault. Those darn ants won't leave them alone. I gave them a little nudge, and they perked up."

The corners of Daniel's mouth turned up in a grin that bordered on laughter, but Rosie didn't mind. She knew he appreciated her gifts.

"I love you, Rosie." He threw an arm around her neck, rubbing his knuckles into the top of her head. "You make my job so much more interesting."

She cringed at the slick sweat that coated his skin. "Ugh, Daniel!" She pushed him away. "Gross! Take a shower!"

Daniel laughed and wiped his sweaty forearm against her neck before he jogged toward the shed, where the other boys were still singing. Daniel and Rosie joked around a lot, but he was normally a very shy, reserved guy. On the rare occasion that he was in a social situation, he didn't talk much.

On the opposite end of the spectrum was loud and exuberant Michael. He liked to be the center of attention and spent a lot of time at local bars. He rode a motorcycle and liked to ride it fast. He was always the one telling the stories that had everyone roaring with laughter. Rosie watched him belting out tunes with Sam and Lucas and smiled. They'd moved on from Alice Cooper and were singing along to the radio, which he'd turned up unreasonably loud.

Simon chose Michael to father the next member of their pack—likely because of his physique—but Michael wasn't exactly champing at the bit to father a child. He wouldn't be raising him alone. Martha would take care of the child while he was a baby, and as he grew, the pack would work together to guide him into adulthood.

"How's my girl?"

Rosie spun on her heel when she heard Stuart's tired old voice call out to her. He approached slowly and unsteadily from the house. He really needed a cane or a walker. She rushed to his side and took his arm.

"Stuart, you should be careful," Rosie said softly. "You'll fall."

"Can barely hear you over that racket," Stuart groused. He turned toward the shed and yelled at the boys. "Turn that noise down! You'll wake the dead!"

Michael rushed to the radio, and the music died down.

Rosie grinned at Stuart, and he winked at her before scowling at the boys.

"Don't you boys have anything better to do than dance around like a bunch of idiots?"

Without another word, Michael went back to processing the deer meat, and Daniel hurried to the back yard. Sam and Lucas kept their heads low.

"I wish you would come to the library and let me read to you some more, Rosie," Stuart said. He took Rosie's hand and squeezed it. "It's been so long. I've got lots of journals with stories you'd love to hear."

"I would love that, Stuart." Rosie squeezed his hand in return. "Now that school is out, I'll have more time. I'll come by for stories more. I promise."

"I'll look forward to it, dear." Stuart turned back toward the house, and Rosie helped him up the porch steps. "I think I've got just enough time for a nap before supper."

Rosie laughed as Stuart disappeared into the house.

"Hey, Rosie, where's my glove?" Sam called out from the shed as Lucas loped off toward the back yard. "Lucas and I are going to play catch."

Rosie frowned. Earlier that spring, she'd had a momentary lapse of judgement and let Becca talk her into trying out for the softball team. She had borrowed Sam's glove. As expected, the tryout was a disaster. She had ducked and covered her head every time the ball came her way. Heat washed over her face as she cringed at the memory.

"I left it out after I used it, and I think Martha put it in the basement." Rosie winced at Sam's scowl. "I'll get it."

Rosie hesitated briefly before she stepped through the front door. She deposited her backpack and shoes in the foyer and made her way through the hall and dining room to the cook's kitchen at the back corner of the house. Past the kitchen, a small doorway led to the basement. She took a deep breath before opening the door. She was too old to be afraid of dusty old basements, yet here she was. The house had been rebuilt a couple of times over the foundation first laid over a hundred years ago. The old, creepy basement remained the same over all that time.

Cavernous walls and a narrow staircase lay before her, and she descended slowly. The cold of the cement stairs seeped through her socks and froze her toes. As she neared the bottom, the blackness that lay before her sent a chill up her spine, and she had to feel around with her toes to find her footing. No light switch had been installed at the top of the stairs, so she was forced to feel around the wall in the dark, looking for the switch at the bottom. When she found it, her stomach jolted with relief, and she couldn't flick it on fast enough. She turned toward the empty expanse of the main room. The dusty cement floor was bare. Shelves lined the walls where years of junk was stored. To the left of the main room, a doorway led to the utility room. To the right, a door hung slightly ajar, and she caught a glimpse of what lay on the other side.

Rosie shook her head. She didn't want to think about that room and what was in it. She focused on the shelves in front of her and purposefully strolled toward the closest box to begin her search. As she passed by the door on the right, a cold breeze touched her cheek, and she shivered. Pausing, she glanced through the door. She'd played in that room numerous times as a child before she was smart enough to be afraid.

Against her better judgment, she reached a hand out and pushed the door all the way open.

A single room. Empty, except for two prison cells. Prison cells. Their home had prison cells. When she was little, playing cops and robbers in what looked like a real jail was so cool. It was a good hiding place in a game of hide and seek, too, second only to the cluttered attic, where decades of keepsakes were packed away.

Rosie moved closer and reached forward, holding a hand over the bars of one cell. She didn't dare touch. Still, the proximity brought forth the ancient emotions trapped there, and they hit her with the force of a freight train. The agony. The total, gutting, unbridled fear. She could feel it. She closed her eyes, and the echoes of screams reached her ears. The terror. The sheer terror.

A sudden, malevolent presence in the room caused her to turn, and she inhaled sharply at the hate-filled eyes staring back at her.

SEVEN

ROSIE

"Amos," Rosie's voice squeaked.

His lip curled in disgust. He moved forward, and she took a step back, finding herself stepping into a cell. Her stomach clenched, and she quickly moved out, away from him and the confines of the prison.

"What are you doing down here?" he demanded.

"I-I was just looking for something." Rosie swallowed and tried her best to straighten her spine. "S-Sam's baseball glove."

A dismissive sigh escaped him as he reached out and touched the bars of one of the cells. The disgust didn't leave his face as he spoke. "It was easier times for the pack when these were used."

Rosie blinked. "What?"

Amos ran his hand up the bars, almost reverently. "Years ago, when these cells were used, things were easier for the pack. They didn't need to worry about loose ends. The pack would choose a recluse. An outcast. Someone who wouldn't be missed. After she gave the pack what it needed, it was done with her. There was never a body to be found. Easy as that." He turned to stare at Rosie. "They ate the bones too. There was nothing left. Every trace of her existence was wiped from this earth. They licked up every last drop of blood from the cement floor."

Rosie shivered. In one of his many rants about pack history, Stuart had told Rosie that the women who mothered their werewolf pups were kept in the cells until after they gave birth. He never said what happened to them after the pups were born, but Rosie had a hunch. She'd heard horror stories about what the Cramer pack did to the women in their house. Amos seemed to delight in filling her in on the details. A cold smile stretched across his lips.

"My father told me about it." Amos looked at Rosie, the intensity of his stare forcing her to take an involuntary step back. "There was a whole ceremony. It was a rite of passage. Every werewolf brought a new member into the pack. Back then, our numbers were impressive." He smiled. "He described the whole ceremony. They watched as she gave birth to your father, and then the pack ate her."

Just when the bile seemed to have settled down into her stomach, it rushed back up her throat. She swallowed, but the sour taste lingered.

"That was the last one. After that, they started sending boys out to big cities, where they could find some junkie or prostitute. They'd put her up in a hotel for nine months and then vanish with the baby after it was born. The pack alpha, my grandfather, said it was more humane. When my father didn't agree, he decided your father would make a better alpha. Look where that got us. Witchcraft and a female werewolf." Amos shook his head. "Women have no place in *our* world. *Our* ceremonies. *Our* traditions." He flicked his eyes toward her. "You're needy. Spoiled. Entitled. Just like the rest of them. They want men to put them on a pedestal and hold doors for them and take care of them, then they screech and cry when they aren't treated as equals."

Amos took a step toward Rosie, making her take another step back. "Now, Simon wants us to pay for our offspring. *Pay* for them. He wants us to *pay* women to give us *our* own offspring."

Rosie swallowed. Her father sought out the services of a Canadian company run by werewolves and for werewolves, which specialized in procuring donor eggs and surrogate mothers. It had been set up under the guidance of the World Werewolf Council. The women didn't know they were offering their services to werewolves, of course, but the company had grown quickly over the last few decades with clientele across the globe. It was becoming the most popular way for werewolves to grow their packs.

Sam was the first werewolf born to the Hart pack from a surrogate mother.

"Inch by inch, our way of life is being destroyed." Amos stared at the bars of the cell as he spoke, a far-off look in his eyes.

Anger bubbled up in Rosie's chest, puddling within her fear like oil in water. "Is change such a bad thing?" Her pathetic squeak of a voice was barely audible. Why couldn't she stop shaking?

Amos turned to her, and she shrank back at the anger emanating from him. "It is when it threatens our existence, the very fabric of our being. You're just a dumb little girl, too absorbed in your own little world. You'll never under-stand what it's like to be part of something so big, so impor-tant. Tradition is what has kept us alive for hundreds of years, and I—"

"Rosie, did you find it?" Sam shouted from the staircase.

Rosie breathed a sigh of relief. "Down here, Sam." She moved into the main room and watched him slowly descend the stairs.

He paused as Amos walked into the main room behind her. "Is everything okay?" His gaze drifted from Rosie to Amos and back again.

Rosie tried her best to look nonchalant and shrugged. "Fine."

"You kids find what you're looking for and get upstairs," Amos said quietly. He moved to the stairs and practically pushed Sam aside as he headed up.

"He's so creepy." Sam rolled his eyes as he hopped down the rest of the stairs.

"You have no idea." Rosie tried her best not to shudder.

Sam eyed Rosie carefully. "He wasn't bothering you, was he? Because if he was giving you a hard time, Dad will take care of it."

As tempting as it was to have her father put Amos in his place, Rosie didn't want to cause drama. She didn't need to add another reason to the ever-growing list of things Amos seemed to hate about her.

"It's fine. He was just giving me a little history lesson."

"Hmm." Sam moved to the shelves and started rummaging through boxes. "Isn't that Stuart's job?"

"Yeah," Rosie mused. She couldn't get what Amos had said out of her head. She'd known the history of those cells to some extent but hadn't realized it'd happened as recently as her father's mother.

Her grandmother.

Breath caught in her throat as the weight of that truth hit her. Her grandmother had been eaten by her family. Stuart would've been there. Did he take part? Did he eat her? The bile churned in her stomach.

Amos was wrong. Change didn't have to be a threat to their existence. *She* was not a threat to their existence. She glanced at Sam and suddenly understood the enormity of what her father was trying to do. Why he pushed Sam so hard.

Sam held the future of their pack in his hands. If Sam didn't move them forward, Amos would drag them back.

EIGHT
SAM

SAMUEL HART STARED AT THE YELLOW NUMBER-TWO pencil as he twisted it between his fingers. He felt the bumps and grooves of the surface under his skin as it moved back and forth, back and forth. He yawned a deep, tired yawn that brought tears to his eyes.

"Sam!" His father snapped at him impatiently.

He dropped the pencil and straightened in his chair.

"Have you been listening to a word I've been saying?" Simon leaned back in his office chair, watching Sam closely from across the top of his large mahogany desk. The glossy finish of the wood's grain reflected the light from the lamp, and pictures of Sam and Rosie sat near its edge. A small tin held a handful of sharpened pencils, and Sam carefully picked up the pencil he'd been holding and put it back with the others.

"Yes, sir." Sam tried to remember the last thing his father had said. He'd stopped paying attention right around the time Simon started lecturing him on how important it was to be respectful to the members of the other pack. The Cramers could kiss his ass. Any respect he had for them had died the day his father brought home Jack's body and broke the news about how he died.

"So, the rogue..." Sam leaned forward and rested his elbows on his knees. He'd been sitting in that chair for almost an hour. "Does William think we know something about it?"

Simon stared at him for a few more seconds before swiveling his chair toward the window and staring out at the blackness of the night. "He said they smelled traces of the rogue in the forest near their house, and it smelled like our pack."

"That's stupid," Sam scoffed. "We've all been here."

"Yeah." Simon looked like he wanted to say something more, but he stopped.

Sam watched his father closely. A look of guilt crossed over Simon's face briefly before he schooled his expression and turned back toward the window. Sam could swear it felt like his father was hiding something, but he shook the thought away.

"You think William is lying?"

Simon hesitated for a moment. "I don't think it's the only reason he asked to meet. He's been asking about Rosie for years. She's sixteen now, time for her to officially be included in pack gatherings. Now, he wants to come and visit."

"You think he's finding an excuse to come here and see Rosie?" Sam's voice rose as a wave of protectiveness flowed over him. William Cramer had a creepy vibe, and Sam didn't like the idea of him sniffing around his sister.

"I can't keep her hidden forever, Sam. The other packs will want to meet her." Simon swiveled his chair back toward Sam, his face a mixture of anger and worry.

Sam could've counted on one finger the number of

times he had seen worry like that on his father's face. "Dad—"

"Most of the pack will be there, Sam. She'll be well protected."

"I don't like it. We should keep her away." Suddenly, he really wished his father hadn't told Michael not to be there. His cousin looked like he could bench-press a bulldozer. No one would dare cross him.

"We have to respect our traditions, Sam."

Sam huffed. "You sound like Amos."

"No...If it were up to Amos, Rosie would be dead."

Sam flinched. The fact that Amos hated Rosie was no secret. Sam had always chalked it up to Amos just being a jackass. "I don't get that. Why?"

"Look," Simon sighed impatiently, "I've tried to shield you and Rosie from it, okay? The truth is the werewolf world you've grown up in and the werewolf world that exists outside our pack are very different. For hundreds of years, werewolves did brutal, barbaric things to women. It's going to take a lot of work to get past that, and most of the werewolf world isn't prepared to accept the arrival of a female werewolf just like that."

Sam flinched at the harsh snap of Simon's fingers as he accentuated his last word. Sam knew the anger on his father's face wasn't directed at him, but he quieted at the harsh tone.

"I've tried my hardest to change that mindset—at least in our pack—for her sake. You and the boys were raised with her. You know her. You accept her." Simon met Sam's gaze, and Sam flinched at the desperation and fear in his eyes.

"Females aren't part of the werewolf world. And witches... Well, that's a whole different level of unknown.

I've tried keeping her witch heritage hidden, but I'm afraid it will get out. The history between werewolves and witches is rocky. I don't know how the Council would react if they knew she was part witch. I'm afraid for her safety."

Sam's stomach somersaulted. His father's fear terrified him. Simon was unflappable, solid, strong. This fearful side of him shook the stable ground Sam walked on. That his fear was of the Council and what they would do to Rosie had Sam even more on edge. He'd never met any of the Council members, but he'd heard stories. On the surface, they were just politicians, but the power they held was terrifying. No one was safe from their wrath. At their fingertips, they had an army of the strongest, fastest werewolves ready to take down any threat at a moment's notice.

"What can we do?"

Simon leaned forward across the desk, resting his arms on the surface. He stared into Sam's eyes. "We need to concentrate on what we can control. Change needs to start here, in our own pack. We can only hope that change will spread."

"The only problem in our pack is Amos. Why can't we just make him leave? He's in your face all the time."

"No." Simon shook his head. "If we banish him, it will only fuel his hatred for Rosie. Out there, banished from the pack, I think he would be a bigger threat. Keeping him close is best."

Sam scoffed.

"No, Sam, listen. I've made that mistake before. If we banish him, we'll be looking over our shoulders all the time." Something flashed in Simon's eyes. Fear? Regret? "We can keep an eye on him here. He won't do anything to Rosie under my nose."

Sam scowled, but he nodded. He still thought they would be better off getting rid of Amos, but as long as his father was around to keep him in line, things would be fine.

NINE

ROSIE

ROSIE LEANED BACK IN THE PASSENGER SEAT OF THE SUV and peered out at the trees. The thick forest thinned out as they approached Hanks Hollow. In the driver's seat, Lucas's head bobbed as he mouthed the words to the upbeat, punky tune blaring through the speakers. It was one of Lucas's favorite bands, and he'd been excited to hear they were playing in town. Usually, the bands that played under the large gazebo in the park were local, but this one was from Chicago. According to Lucas, their drummer had grown up in the area. They were scheduled to play in Madison that weekend and decided to do a Wednesday night show for the locals. Tourist season was in full swing, so they were sure to have a crowd.

"I'm psyched about seeing these guys. I think you'll like them." Lucas always got excited when he talked about music he liked. His enthusiasm left a warm feeling in the pit of Rosie's stomach, and she couldn't help the wide smile that spread across her face.

"I'm sure they'll be great," Rosie said. "Even if they

aren't, ice cream from The Sconnie Scoop will be worth the trip all by itself."

The ice cream store had the tastiest sugar-sprinkled cones, and they were on Main Street, right across from the park. Most of the snack shops were strategically located to lure tourists to buy treats to enjoy while they sat on the grass and listened to music.

Lucas rolled his eyes, and his shoulders shook with laughter. "I swear, Rosie, you'll turn any event into an excuse to eat."

Rosie rolled her eyes and batted at his arm. The song blaring through the speakers was catchy. It sounded exactly like something Lucas would listen to. She tried to imagine the song playing for the old people and young families that would make up the tourist crowd, and she wrinkled her nose. "The band is really good, but are they a little edgy for the tourist crowd?"

"Yeah, you won't hear much of this tonight, I'm sure." Lucas frowned. "They started off as a cover band, so they'll probably stick with the crowd pleasers, for the most part."

"You don't sound excited about that."

Lucas glanced at Rosie as he pulled into a parking space across from the park. "They'll still sound great. I was just hoping to hear more of their original music. If I could go down to Madison to see them this weekend, I would. But Dad would never let me. And even if he did, I don't think your dad would."

"That's true. He's pretty partial to keeping the pack close." Rosie glanced out the window toward the park. In the center of the green expanse of grass, the band was hauling equipment up to the gazebo stage to set up for the night. Nearby, the village maintenance manager was carrying an armload of firewood. "Nice! Looks like they're planning to light the pit tonight."

Most nights from May through October, the village lit an enormous firepit. Locals and tourists mingled in front of the glow of the fire as they listened to music. A beer garden was set up nearby.

"First things first," Lucas said as he opened his door. "We need to get you some food. I know you'll stand around staring at the shops until we do."

Rosie rolled her eyes as she hopped out of the SUV and joined Lucas on the sidewalk. "Ice cream first. Then some popcorn."

"Yes, ma'am."

Lucas chuckled as Rosie kicked at him. They headed toward Main Street and into The Sconnie Scoop. Only a few customers lingered in the store, and Rosie quickly browsed the menu before ordering a double-scoop vanilla cone with sprinkles. She glanced at Lucas, who was watching her with a small smirk.

"You're not getting anything?" she asked.

Lucas shook his head.

"Suit yourself. I'm not sharing, though, so if you want some, now's the time." After Lucas shook his head again, she fished her father's credit card out of her pocket and handed it to the clerk. She licked at her cone and peered at Lucas out of the corner of her eye. "You're not going to stand around watching me eat now, are you? That's creepy."

"Fine, I won't watch." Lucas laughed as he strolled toward the door. He held it open for her as she stepped through, out into the orange glow of the setting sun. "The band is still setting up. You want to go get your popcorn now?"

"Okay." The word was muffled as Rosie took in a

mouthful of ice cream.

As they entered the popcorn shop, old Peggy Branson's bright voice greeted them. "Rosie! How are you doing, doll? It's been so long!"

Lucas leaned forward and mumbled into her ear. "They know you by name here? That's a little sad, Rosie."

Rosie elbowed Lucas in the ribs. "Hi, Mrs. Branson! I'm good. Just came by for a box of cheese popcorn. How's Emily?"

"Oh, she's great! She's so glad to be done with school. Do you girls ever play together? I haven't seen you in so long." Mrs. Branson scooped popcorn into a box.

Lucas snorted, and Rosie elbowed him again.

"Oh, I think we've outgrown the playing, but I still see her at school sometimes." Rosie left out the fact that Mrs. Branson's granddaughter ignored Rosie at school. They hadn't played together in years.

"That'll be three fifty, dear." Mrs. Branson rang the card through and handed it back. "You tell that handsome father of yours that I say hi." A mischievous grin crossed the old woman's face.

"I sure will, Mrs. Branson. Thank you!" Rosie pushed Lucas as he started to laugh and was thankful that he waited until they got outside before he doubled over in hysterics.

"You're awful, Lucas," Rosie scolded. "She's an old woman. We'll all be old someday—just remember that."

They crossed the street to the park, and Lucas's laughter didn't die down until they were trudging across the freshly mowed grass toward the gazebo. Small clusters of bushes and blooms dotted the landscape, and crabapple trees filled the air with the sweet scent of their spring blossoms.

When the band started to play, a fire was roaring in the firepit. People laid out blankets or sat in the grass to munch on treats and enjoy the music. Some took seats on the benches placed around the gazebo and firepit. Some sat at picnic tables and ate brats. Rosie and Lucas found a spot in the grass not far from the stage.

"Last chance," Rosie said as she finished off the ice cream cone. "There's one bite left."

"It's just the cone," Lucas whined. "There isn't even any ice cream in it."

"Hey, you had your chance, buddy." Rosie popped the last bite into her mouth as the band started playing "Sweet Caroline."

The band played several more classics over the course of the evening, but they put a faster, punk-like twist on the songs. Rosie loved it. She could see why Lucas wanted to come so badly, and she was really glad she'd joined him.

As they sat in the grass and shared the box of popcorn, she caught herself staring at him more than once. The delight and fascination on his face was hard not to watch. His blue eyes lit up with joy, and a small smile played at his lips. She closed her eyes and tried opening herself up to his energy. She could tell he was happy, but that was all. She just couldn't get a full read of him. It had been that way since the day she healed him. Her grandmother had healed dozens of people and never had trouble reading their energy afterward, so Rosie had no clue why she couldn't read Lucas now. Maybe something was wrong with her.

"You okay?"

Rosie opened her eyes to find him staring at her, his head cocked to one side and his brow raised in amusement. Heat rushed to her cheeks. She must have looked ridiculous, sitting there with her eyes closed.

"Yeah," she said. "Just enjoying the music. You were right. They're great."

A bright smile stretched across his face. "Right?"

As he focused on the stage again, a strand of hair fell into his eyes, and Rosie fought the urge to reach up and brush it away. It looked so soft. She bit her lip.

"I'm getting cold. I'm going to go sit by the fire." Rosie started to get up, and Lucas leaped to his feet.

"I'll come with you."

They headed over to the firepit. After taking a spot on one of the benches, Rosie held her hands up to the fire to warm them.

Lucas cleared his throat. "Thank you for coming with me tonight."

"Of course. I like hearing the bands you listen to. I always end up liking them."

"It's more than that," Lucas said. "You always have my back."

Warmth spread through Rosie's body. "And you always have mine. Remember the time when we were little, and I fell down that muddy embankment and got stuck?"

Lucas smiled, clearly remembering.

"You stayed with me for hours, waiting for help," Rosie said. "You talked to me the whole time so that I wouldn't be afraid."

"I remember," Lucas said. "Remember the time I got hit in the face with porcupine quills?" His face scrunched up as though he was remembering the pain.

Rosie remembered that day well. It was the first time she'd ever used her energy to heal. Her grandma had told her the energy would come to her when she needed it, and she would just know. Her grandma had been right.

TEN

ROSIE

Rosie had been eight years old. They were playing hunters and prey. She could still hear Sammy's voice in her head.

"I said no girls allowed!"

The shouted telepathic words had stung. Werewolf telepathy wasn't much different from a verbal conversation —the voices, the inflection, everything sounded the same.

"That's not fair, Sammy!"

If she were in human form, Rosie would have been stomping her feet and crying. In wolf form, her ears were flat against her head, and her wolf sounds alternated between a low growl and a pathetic whimper. Unlike the other wolves of the pack, who bore the gray, brown, and black markings of a typical gray wolf, Rosie's fur was bright red, just like her hair.

"Just let her play, Sam," Lucas reasoned impatiently. *"She won't leave us alone until we do."*

"No way!" Sam complained. *"Last time, she used her freaky witch magic. That's cheating!"*

"I won't use it this time," she lied. *"I promise!"*

That really wasn't a promise she could keep. Trying not to use her magic was like trying not to breathe. It just happened.

"What's all the commotion over here?" Jack strolled into the clearing, dead leaves crunching under his enormous paws. Daniel and Michael bounced along behind him.

"Sammy won't let me play." Rosie wasn't above tattling. Being the only girl and the youngest in the pack forced her hand sometimes.

"She cheats!" Sam yelled as he growled at his sister, baring his teeth. *"She uses her magic to find us."*

"Well..." Jack drew out the word slowly, thinking. *"Is that really cheating, though? The point of playing hunters and prey is to use your skills as a hunter to find your prey. Rosie has a few extra skills. That just means you need to figure out how to outsmart her."*

Letting out a frustrated growl, Sam snapped his teeth at Rosie angrily, and quick as a wink, Daniel and Michael jumped to her defense, leaping in front of her and baring their teeth at Sam. Rosie sat up a little straighter behind them, and Sam shrank down to the ground, tucking in his tail. The threat was harmless, really. They knew Sam would never hurt her, but they liked to hold the fact that they were older and larger over Sam and Lucas. Protecting Rosie now and then, when playing got too rough, gave them an excellent opportunity to do that.

"Hey now!" Jack snapped. His words scolded, but Rosie heard a smile in the light tone. *"Everyone calm down and play nicely. And Sam..."* Jack focused his attention on Sam, giving him a hard stare. *"No one is excluded from our games. Right?"*

"Right," Sam grumbled.

"Are you guys going to play with us?" Rosie hopped up and down, trying to nip at Daniel's ears. Daniel and Michael hardly ever played anymore.

"Jeez, Rosie." Michael batted her away playfully, and she tumbled head over heels across the ground like a lopsided ball. Michael puffed his chest out, raising his head proudly. *"You know we're too old for these baby games. We're real hunters now."*

At thirteen and twelve, Daniel and Michael were old enough to be included when the pack ventured out together on hunts. Daniel had made his first kill only a few months ago. Sam, Lucas, and Rosie played games to sharpen their skills, but they still had baby teeth that weren't strong enough to sink into real prey. The real growth spurt when a werewolf pup developed into a young adult happened around ten years old.

"Let us know if they give you any more trouble, Rosie." Daniel gave Sam and Lucas a warning growl as he and Michael followed Jack back toward the house.

"Come on, Rosie," Sam huffed. *"You can be hunter."*

It was a peace offering. Being hunter was the best part of the game. *"Thanks, Sammy."*

She pounced on his back, and he rolled over, knocking her to the ground in a tackle. Lucas made a loud war cry before he took a flying leap onto Sam's back, and the three of them rolled around in the dirt, their nipping and swatting punctuated by playful growls.

It was then that Rosie felt a new presence in the grass, not far away. She felt the energy of the plants and animals around her all the time. Each living being had its own unique energy. A raccoon felt different from a deer. A tree felt different from a wildflower. She felt them all, but she hadn't felt this strange energy before. Drawn in, she left the playful brawl and wandered off toward it, sniffing at the air.

"*Where are you going?*" Sam whined. "*I thought you wanted to play.*"

"*She hears something,*" Lucas said. "*I hear it too.*"

She didn't bother correcting Lucas. She didn't want to explain to him that she felt the creature's energy before she heard it. Rosie didn't talk about her witch magic often. It only made her feel further isolated from the pack.

Sam and Lucas hunched down into a stalking stance, laying their ears back flat and baring their teeth. Low growls rumbled in their throats. They approached on either side of Rosie, boxing in the creature making its way through the tall grass, the long blades swaying with its movement. Suddenly, the creature jumped out of the grass in front of them. Rosie yelped and scrambled backward. The creature halted in front of them, hissing and raising its quills.

"*Is that a porcupine?*" Lucas asked as he sat up and sniffed the air. "*I've never seen one up close before.*"

Rosie lowered her head and sniffed cautiously at the ground. The creature cowered and skittered backward.

"*It looks like Rosie after she wakes up in the morning.*" Lucas giggled.

She growled at him and nipped at his foot as he laughed, but she knew that wasn't far from the truth. In her human form, Rosie's hair looked like a tangled scarlet-colored rat's nest in the morning.

Sam crept forward and batted carefully at the porcupine. It shifted, stomping its feet on the ground and hissing. Its quills quivered, and Rosie couldn't suppress the urge to laugh with Sam and Lucas at the unusual display.

Lucas moved forward and raised a paw to bat at it again,

and Rosie felt the porcupine's energy suddenly turn dangerously defensive.

"*Lucas, wait!*" she called out, but she was too late.

The porcupine turned and swatted its tail straight into his face. Lucas let out a sharp yelp of pain and howled as he hid his head under his paws. The porcupine waddled quickly back into the grass as Sam and Rosie rushed to Lucas's side.

"*Get it out!*" he cried, pawing at his face frantically. A dozen sharp needles had punctured his fur like a pincushion.

"*Sammy, go get help!*" Rosie shouted before shifting to human form.

Long, unruly curls hung loosely over her bare chest as she hunched over Lucas. Behind her, Sam bolted for the house. Pain-filled whimpers vibrated in Lucas's throat, and her heart ached. Hurt and fear rolled off him in waves, and the intensity overwhelmed her. She didn't know much about porcupines, and though she didn't think their quills were poisonous, she wasn't about to wait around and find out.

Her fingers were surprisingly steady as she ran them over his face. The quills were deep, and as she pulled at the first one, Lucas cried out and thrashed under her hands. Rosie closed her eyes and took a few deep breaths. When she could feel her calm winning over the fear and hurt, she let the energy pour out of herself as she stroked his fur, immediately feeling his muscles relax. She resumed trying to pull the quills out of his face, but they wouldn't budge. His breath stuttered in pain-filled panting for a few moments before he changed to human form.

"It hurts so bad, Rosie," he whimpered. Around the

trails of tear tracks, the quills were deeply embedded in his cheeks.

That was when Rosie felt it. When she closed her eyes, she could visualize a glowing red ember of healing energy inside herself, begging to be released. She opened her eyes and stared down into Lucas's tear-filled eyes. "Don't be afraid," she whispered as she placed her hands on his cheeks.

She closed her eyes and visualized the energy pouring through her hands and out through her fingertips. The tingling hum of an electric charge ran between them, and after a few moments, he gasped. Her eyes shot open, and she hesitantly looked down at his face and sucked in a sharp breath. The quills had fallen away and lay scattered on the ground. The puncture wounds were gone. Shock and confusion replaced the pain in his eyes.

"Rosie?"

She looked up, startled, at the sound of her father's voice. There, standing in human form, were Simon, Jack, Roger, and Amos. Sam stood off to one side, his eyes like saucers.

It wasn't a secret among the members of the pack that she was half witch, and her grandma had told her father what Rosie was capable of. Still, she didn't think anyone, herself included, really believed she could heal someone before that day. They all wore various expressions of disbelief—all except Amos, who looked at her with vicious contempt. If she'd been afraid of him before, she was terrified of him now.

Their emotions hung in the air, and she choked on them as she struggled to take in a deep breath. Amos's hatred was palpable, practically leaving a raw, open wound on her skin.

The others' lingering emotions were like salt in the open wound—uncertainty...*fear*.

"Daddy?" It was a plea.

He stood still, staring at her as if she was a stranger.

Roger seemed to snap out of his shock first, and he rushed forward to check on his son.

"Thank you, Rosie," he said, giving her an uneasy smile. "Come on, Lucas, let's go."

Lucas looked at Rosie with an unreadable expression before he and his father both shifted. Roger, in wolf form, bit down on the fuzzy scruff of Lucas's neck and picked him up. Lucas dangled in his father's hold, his eyes still on Rosie as Roger carried him off toward the house.

"Simon." Amos's voice was low and angry. "This isn't right. *She* isn't right. We should have listened to Frank. She's an abomination—"

Rosie flinched, and her cheeks heated with shame. She didn't know who Frank was, but *abomination* didn't sound like a good thing. Frank didn't sound like someone friendly.

"Enough!" Simon turned on Amos quickly. Amos took a step back and bowed his head.

"Jack, take Rosie and Sammy back to the house. Now." Simon's voice left no room for argument.

Jack, Sam, and Rosie quickly changed to wolf form and started toward the house at a slow jog. Behind them, Rosie could hear an argument start.

"What would the Council say, Simon?"

"I said enough, Amos!" Simon's angry voice had been steady and powerful. "She is my daughter and a member of this pack. She will be a member of this pack as long as I'm alpha."

~

Rosie took a deep breath and shook her head, the memories of that day dissipating like a picture on an Etch A Sketch.

"You put your hands on my face, and the pain disappeared." The heaviness of Lucas's stare weighed on Rosie, and she felt the need to lighten the mood.

"Neither of us has gone near another porcupine," she said with a laugh. "Lesson learned."

Lucas frowned at her deflection.

Rosie held her hands out toward the flames again, trying to warm them.

"It's not that cold out," Lucas teased as he grabbed one of her hands. "Jeez! Your hands are freezing!"

"I told you I was cold," Rosie groused.

Lucas covered her hands with his, rubbing back and forth to warm them. As they touched, electricity tingled in her fingers and traveled up her arms. The pleasure was more than she could ever describe. Her cheeks warmed as she glanced at him. He watched her, his blue eyes piercing. The glow of the fire cast a mixture of light and shadow across his face. Did he feel the tingle too? She'd felt it before, when she touched him. It was probably just her, another one of her freaky witch things. She didn't want to ask him. He would think she was being silly.

After a few moments, she realized they'd been staring into each other's eyes for a long time, and a wave of self-consciousness ran through her. She pulled her hands away and shifted her gaze back to the fire.

A moment passed before Lucas cleared his throat. "We can go now if you want. I think they're almost done for the night."

"Are you sure? Do you want to go get their autographs or something?"

Lucas laughed. "I'm not a groupie, Rosie. I just like their music."

Feeling like she'd asked a stupid question, Rosie shrugged and mumbled under her breath, "I would want an autograph if I were you."

"Well, you're not me." Lucas smiled. "Come on. Let's go home."

ELEVEN
ROSIE

Rosie was still humming "Sweet Caroline" an hour later as she strolled down the hall toward the kitchen. Shouts from the rec room grabbed her attention, and she paused to find out what the commotion was. She expected to see Sam and Lucas betting on Mario Kart again, but instead, she found Michael and Daniel in the midst of a game of pool.

"Rosie!" Daniel called out to her as Michael took a long swig of beer. "Come in and play referee. Michael is cheating."

"I'm not cheating!" Michael threw his arms up in the air.

"How do you cheat at pool?" Rosie asked, crossing her arms.

"Exactly! Thank you, Rosie!" Michael hopped across the room and pulled her into a one-armed hug. "You've always been my favorite."

"Michael..." Rosie pushed him away with a laugh. He smelled like a brewery. "I'm not saying you're not cheating.

I'm asking how you're cheating. If there is a way to cheat at pool, you'll find it."

"Oh, my heart!" Michael clutched his chest, feigning a heart attack.

Rosie blew him a kiss. "I'm going to make some hot chocolate, and then I'm going to bed."

"Good night, Rosie," Daniel called with a little wave.

Michael pulled her back in for another one-armed hug and kissed the top of her head before she shuffled off to the kitchen.

Reaching up to the cupboard for her favorite mug, she pulled it out and took it to the sink, filled it with tap water, then put it into the microwave to warm it. She went to the pantry and sifted through the contents until she found a box of instant cocoa mix. She leaned against the counter, humming "Sweet Caroline," until the microwave beeped. After pulling one sleeve over her hand to shield her fingers from the hot mug, she took it from the microwave and put it on the counter. As she stirred the hot chocolate mixture into her mug, she glanced out the window and noticed the patio lights were on. Sitting outside with her hot chocolate sounded nice, so she headed through the dining room to the patio door. She peeked through the glass and spotted Stuart sitting at the patio table, peering out at the trees. She paused for a moment. Was she ready to talk to him? She'd been avoiding him ever since Amos told her about her grandmother.

Her hand seemed to turn the doorknob of its own volition. Guess she had her answer. She stepped outside onto the stone surface as Stuart turned in his seat to look at her.

"Hello, Rosie." He gave a brief smile before patting the chair next to him. "How's my girl?"

"I'm okay." Rosie crossed the patio and sat down in an empty seat across from Stuart. "It's a nice night."

A quiet hum was the only response from her great uncle. Rosie bit her lip. Did she want to open this can of worms? It seemed better to leave it be and keep the peace that denial of the past afforded them.

But something in her screamed. She had to know if the gentle old man she'd loved all these years was the cold-blooded killer Amos had described.

"Amos told me something." The words squeaked out of Rosie's mouth. She turned her gaze to her cup of hot chocolate and stared into the liquid, asking it for the courage to continue. "He said that the pack killed my grandmother. Is that true?"

The words were out. The conversation was started. She couldn't go back now.

"It's true, child." Stuart's reply was soft.

She glanced at him. He continued studying the trees, and she was thankful. Not having to meet his eyes when she asked the next question would make it much easier.

"Were you there? Did you...eat her?"

Stuart closed his eyes. "It was a long time ago, Rosie. Times were different."

"But...you did, didn't you?" Tears pricked Rosie's eyes, and she swallowed the emotion swelling in her throat.

"Yes."

The tears spilled down her cheeks. "Stuart..." She paused. What could she possibly say to that?

Stuart finally turned his gaze back to Rosie. "Amos shouldn't have told you that. It wasn't his place. Things are much different now, Rosie. The pack would never dream of doing something like that anymore. Your father would never let that happen. And when he's alpha, Sam won't either."

Rosie swallowed again and nodded. "I know."

"I wish there was something I could say to make this better, but there isn't. I'm sorry." Another tear slipped down her cheek, and she felt Stuart's anger from across the table. "Damn Amos. Why did he have to go and tell you that? And I'm willing to bet he was none too gentle about it, either."

Stuart's shaky hand reached across the table and clasped Rosie's. His skin was warm and soft. Though tears still glistened in her eyes, Rosie forced a smile. Inside, her stomach churned. The sweet, gentle image of Stuart was forever changed in her mind.

TWELVE
LUCAS

"Rosie, you landed on Park Place." Sam scowled and crossed his arms. "You have to pay me."

"If you own Park Place, where's the card? I don't see it in front of you," Rosie shot back.

"You took it, you cheater! You must have!"

Rosie *had* taken the card. Lucas had pretended to be watching television while she did it minutes earlier when Sam got up to go to the bathroom. She'd shoved it back into the pile of cards on the middle of the board. Lucas didn't really care. He hadn't wanted to play Monopoly in the first place.

"Ugh." Rosie threw her arms up in the air. "The only reason we're playing this stupid game is because Dad caught you betting on Mario Kart with Michael and took the Nintendo away. I told you to stop doing that!"

"Fine!" Sam got up from the floor and knocked the board off the coffee table. "Play something else then. I'm going to bed."

Sam stormed out of the room. Moments later, his footsteps could be heard pounding up the stairs then across the upstairs hallway before his bedroom door slammed shut. Somewhere in the house, Simon shouted out a warning to *stop slamming doors!*

Lucas looked at the mess of game pieces and cards and the overturned game board then swiveled his gaze to Rosie. She was still sitting on the floor, her face tense. Her eyes darted toward him, and Lucas jumped at the malice directed his way.

"What?" She snapped.

"Nothing," Lucas whispered.

Rosie had been in a crappy mood all day. It had rubbed off on Sam, which prompted the bickering. The two of them had fought before. In what world did siblings not fight? But they usually made up pretty quickly. More often than not, it was Rosie who came around then used her magic to calm Sam.

When Lucas had started his day, he'd been determined to tell Rosie how he felt about her. Last night at the park, something had happened between them. He'd seen the old Rosie instead of the one who'd been hiding from him for the past year. But his plans had been crushed when she sulked through breakfast, picked a fight with Sam, then disappeared into the woods for the rest of the day.

Choosing not to say anything to draw Rosie's wrath, Lucas turned his attention back to the mess on the floor and started picking up the game pieces and cards. He started putting the pieces back into the box and heard Rosie huff out a deep sigh.

"I'm sorry," Rosie said. "Let me help."

She scooted around the coffee table, and as she leaned over to help him, Lucas glanced at her face. He was surprised to see a tear sliding down her cheek. Without thinking, he reached forward and caught the tear, wiping it away with his thumb.

Rosie flinched then looked at him. Her wine-colored eyes widened for a moment then lowered to the floor as she sat back on her heels. She cleared her throat. "Did you know that werewolves used to eat the women who carried their babies?"

Lucas was caught off guard. Of all the things for her to say at that moment, he never would have bet on that.

"Yeah." Lucas rubbed his forehead. "My dad told me. It was a long time ago though. Most packs stopped doing that decades ago. I don't think there are many packs that do it anymore."

Her head snapped up, and her eyes held a fire Lucas had never seen. "There are still packs that do it now?"

"Well...I'm not sure," Lucas said honestly. "I don't think so?" He shrugged.

"It's so sick." Rosie bit her lip and another tear dripped down her cheek. "Did you know that my *grandmother* was eaten by the pack? Lucas, Stuart was there. He took part in it. How messed up is that?"

"Jesus!"

"I know!" Rosie sniffed. "I mean, what am I supposed to do with that? All these years, he's treated me like I was his special girl, but I can't get the image of him as a killer out of my head. How could he do that to another person? And how can I ever look at him the same way?"

Lucas thought for a moment, trying to be careful how he answered. "He's still the same person he was before you found out. It's messed up, but things were different back then. My dad said werewolves hated women. I'm not really sure why. Something to do with witches. I'm guessing he's not the same person he was before things changed."

Rosie sighed. "Right."

"You're not afraid of him, are you?" Lucas hoped not. They all lived in fear that the Council would one day decide to take Rosie away...or take her life. No one talked about it. Lucas wasn't sure if she grasped how much danger she was in, or if she *did* grasp it and had just learned to live with it and hide her fear. He hated thinking that on top of fearing the Council, she would now have to fear going to sleep in her own home.

Relief coursed through him when a small smile ticked at her lips. "I'm not afraid of Stuart."

"Right? I mean, come on," Lucas chuckled and nudged her. "Can you imagine him hurting anyone? I don't think you'd have any trouble outrunning him, anyway. Slugs move faster."

Rosie snorted then wiped at her eyes. "I need to talk about something else. Are you excited about the party?"

Lucas tried not to be hurt by the way her face brightened at the mention of the party. What did she see in Mason? Didn't she see what a jerk he was? "You're still going? I thought maybe since your dad told you to stay away from Mason—"

"He'll come around," Rosie said. She grinned and started cleaning up the Monopoly game. "Once he gets to know Mason the way I know him, he'll be fine with it."

"I don't know," Lucas shook his head. "He really seems to hate his father."

Rosie blinked at him. "Exactly. His father. Not him. I just wish I was seeing him somewhere other than a party. I don't even know what people do at parties." She bit her lip. "You've been to a few parties, right? What do you usually do?"

Lucas rolled his eyes. "They really kind of suck. People

get drunk and stupid. The music is always too loud, yet everyone still always tries to kill time by spreading gossip. Last year's party was all about Cassie Barnes."

"Ugh." Rosie winced. "I've never liked Cassie. She's always treated me like crap. I still felt bad for her. No one ever talks to me, so I don't really know what the gossip was about. I don't really care. I just know that every time I was in the same room with her, I wanted to cry. Her sadness was so strong I could feel it in my bones. Whoever was spreading rumors about her is evil."

The last of the Monopoly pieces had been cleaned up, and Lucas picked up the board and put it into the box then placed the lid on top. He thought carefully for a moment. This was his chance to tell her. She'd hate him...but she needed to know. He cleared his throat. "Actually—"

"What are you still doing up?" Simon's voice made Lucas jump. "Just because you don't have school in the morning doesn't mean you can stay up all night."

"Sorry, Dad." Rosie picked up the game and stood. She crossed the room to the cabinet in the corner where dozens of other games were kept.

"You too, Lucas," Simon said. "I know your dad said the two of you need to get on the road early in the morning. You're going fishing, right?"

"Fishing." Lucas nodded. Fishing...camping...Roger always gave Simon some line about father-son bonding time when they left town to go meet up with the other Becketts. Letting Simon know where they were actually going would put him in a bad spot. As alpha, Simon would be obligated to tell Marcus about what they were doing. It was better to keep him in the dark.

"Goodnight, Lucas." Rosie's fingers brushed the top of Lucas's head as she walked by.

Lucas turned toward the hall where Simon stared at him expectantly. He tried not to be angry at his alpha. How could Simon know he'd ruined Lucas's chance to tell Rosie that the person who spread the worst kind of rumors about Cassie Barnes was Mason Lewis?

THIRTEEN
LUCAS

Roger's sleek Lexus tumbled over the rough highway. The smooth ride the sedan normally boasted was no match for the rough Wisconsin roads after winter had taken its toll. Cracks and potholes covered the pavement, and every once in a while, Roger would hiss as though sympathizing with a physical pain the potholes were inflicting upon his car. Soon, men in orange hats would come and fill in the cracks before winter came and messed everything up again.

Towering trees gave way to open fields as they drove southeast toward the farmland at the southern part of Beckett territory. Open skies stretched over rolling hills that looked like a blanket billowing in the breeze. Pastures of roaming cattle and endless fields of wheat and corn dotted the landscape. As beautiful as it was, this drive always filled Lucas with anxiety. The wolf in him craved the cover of trees. The open landscape that lay out before them provided nothing to hunt and nowhere to hide.

Part of what made the Beckett Brewery famous was home-grown ingredients. Though several hundred acres of farmland south of the Beckett territory were owned by the Becketts, pack members were rarely there—only often enough to check up on things. The fields were farmed by hired hands who knew the Beckett brewery business well but knew nothing about the secrets of the family behind the name.

Albertville was a small farming town in the vicinity of the Becketts' farmland, but even calling it a town was generous. A grain mill, a general store, a farm-equipment dealership, and a few houses dotted the roadside along a stretch of highway. The Wild Boar was a little tavern the locals frequented. Lucas and Roger had joined the other Becketts at The Wild Boar the first Monday of every month for as long as Lucas could remember. He knew the owners and many of the locals by name, including the farmers who worked the Beckett fields.

Roger pulled the car into the gravel parking lot alongside the tavern. The door of the bar flew open, and a tall man ducked through the doorway and lumbered across the lot toward them. At over six and a half feet tall, Shawn Beckett had a few inches on Roger, and his lean, muscular build was larger than Roger's scrawny form. Otherwise, they could have passed as twins. Blue eyes, brown hair, chiseled features—the Beckett genes were easy to spot. Though his large form looked intimidating, Shawn wouldn't hurt a fly. He was much more likely to break up a fight than start one.

Behind him, Christopher and Travis followed. Though Christopher's age was creeping up on him, turning his dark hair gray and weathering his skin, his long legs still carried him forward with powerful momentum. His son, Travis, was about Roger's height with red hair and blue eyes that held a bit of mischief.

Lucas barely had the passenger door open before Shawn dragged him out of the car and into his arms. "Lucas! It's good to see you, kid! You're getting taller every time I see you."

As Shawn ruffled Lucas's hair, he couldn't fight his smile as he hugged his uncle back. "Hey, Shawn. I missed you."

Shawn pulled away and turned toward Roger, giving his brother a tight embrace. "Hey, brother. How are you?"

"Can't complain. How are you doing, Shawn?"

"I'll be better after a burger and a beer. Let's get inside."

After hugs with Christopher and Travis, the Beckett clan moved out of the sunlight and into the darkness of the tavern, where they were met by a chorus of cheerful greetings. A few men were sitting at the bar, but most had congregated at the tables, where they ate lunch and talked, creating a sea of weathered faces, flannel shirts, and trucker's hats advertising seed companies. The only woman in the room stood behind the bar. Tight gray curls framed a small face that lit up when she spotted Lucas.

"Hey, Vern!" she yelled to her husband in the kitchen as she scooted herself around the end of the bar and shuffled across the floor toward Lucas. The rasp in her voice and the tight lines around her mouth were evidence of years of smoking. "The Becketts are here. Put some burgers on for them." As she approached, she pulled Lucas into a hug. "How are you doing, kiddo? Getting taller every day, I see. You're going to catch up to your uncle Shawn before too long."

Lucas smiled at the old woman when she kissed his cheek. She smelled like cigarettes, kitchen grease, and alcohol.

"Hey, Ethel, why don't you grab us a few glasses of what

you have on tap." Shawn smiled as he clapped Lucas on the back.

"The watered-down piss water I have on tap is for the locals, not you beer snobs." Ethel winked. "But I think I can find something for you in the back."

She disappeared into the back room as the Becketts settled down at one of the tables. Minutes later, she came back out with five bottles of a local IPA and glasses.

When she placed them on the table, Shawn nodded his approval. "Nice choice, Ethel." He looked at Lucas. "Okay, kid. Give it a try."

Lucas reached for a bottle. The fact that he was a sixteen-year-old kid being encouraged to sample beer said a lot about the people he was with. No one batted an eye. He'd been doing this for years. He poured it into his glass and swirled it around before taking a tentative sniff. Cupping a hand over the top of the glass to warm it, he swirled some more then took another sniff. His keen wolf senses detected malted grains, tangerine and citrus hops, and fermented yeast. He tipped the glass up to the light and made a show of looking at the hazy liquid. He took a small sip and let the taste linger on his tongue before he swallowed. "Definitely citrus hops. It's not bad."

"It's a newer microbrewery out of Madison. They're growing. Just moved from a little operation downtown to a bigger brewhouse." Shawn studied the label before taking another drink from his bottle. "Wouldn't mind dropping in on them next time I'm down there."

Lucas nodded as he took another sip. Every visit with Shawn included beer tasting and education. Shawn was well known in the Wisconsin craft-brew community. He knew his stuff and was happy to pass the knowledge on to

Lucas. And Lucas was happy to learn. His uncle had the coolest job in the world.

"Make sure you bring back some free samples. I like this one." Travis smiled as he took a long pull from his bottle, foregoing the glass.

Travis wasn't into the beer-tasting experience the way Shawn and Christopher were. He didn't know the craft as well as Shawn did, but he was great at managing the brewery. The workers loved him.

After an hour of eating burgers and cheese curds and talking with the farmers, Shawn drained the last of his third beer. "All right, boys. Time to talk shop." He glanced toward the bar and called out to Ethel, who was chatting with some of her regulars. "Hey, Ethel, can we use your office?"

"Sure thing, Shawn."

Normally, this was the part of the visit where Shawn and Roger would disappear into the office, shut the door, and talk about pack business. Sometimes Lucas joined them, but he usually stayed out in the bar area and played euchre with Travis, Christopher, and Ethel.

Standing from the table, Shawn nodded toward the office behind the bar and nudged Lucas's shoulder. Guess they wanted him to join them. He fought a sigh. Playing cards sounded much more fun than talking about pack business.

He stood and followed his father and his uncle to the little office, which reeked of cigarette smoke. A desk in the corner was buried beneath a pile of papers. Shawn took a seat in the desk chair and nodded toward the table and chairs on the opposite wall. Roger and Lucas each took a seat. As Shawn droned on about gross earnings and tax write-offs, Lucas's gaze wandered around the room.

Ashtrays, unopened bills, and old beer cans covered the table next to him. He fished his phone out of his pocket and started scrolling through Reddit.

"Pay attention, Lucas."

Suppressing a groan, Lucas stuffed his phone back in his pocket. "Sorry."

Roger sighed. "You need to know this stuff, Lucas."

"Why?" Lucas looked from his father to Shawn.

Shawn glanced at Roger. "It's time to have this conversation, Roger."

Roger looked at Lucas and back at Shawn, then he nodded.

Shawn leaned forward, propping his elbows on his knees and clasping his hands together. "You need to be ready to take over, Lucas. Our pack is going to need an alpha. Soon. I'm next in line, but I can't run both the pack and the brewery business. My place is out on the road, marketing our brand, keeping up on the trade. Marcus's son is next in line behind me, but he's ten years old. Marcus is almost sixty, and his health isn't great. You do the math."

A cold lump of dread settled in his stomach. "What about Travis?"

"I love Travis. Everyone loves Travis. But he's not alpha material. Christopher is in his fifties. We're out of options."

The horror Lucas felt must have shown on his face, judging by Shawn's disappointed frown. Lucas swallowed, finding his voice. "What about the Harts?"

"The Harts have been good to us." Roger lowered his head as he spoke. "I would do anything for them, but they aren't our pack."

"Dad, my life is there."

"You have no future there, Lucas. You could have a future with the Becketts." Roger looked at Lucas closely. "You're my son, and you're so much stronger and wiser than I could have ever dreamed. You have it in you to lead our pack. I want that for you. And I can't give it to you there. You know only someone in the family line can be chosen as alpha."

The future alpha of a pack was chosen by the current alpha. Usually, that was the alpha's son, sometimes a nephew or a cousin, but always a member of the family. The alpha was the family member who was the strongest, the smartest—the one with the ability to lead.

Lucas ran a hand through his hair and pulled at the collar of his T-shirt. The heavy smell of cigarette smoke was starting to suffocate him. "I haven't been named a successor by Marcus. I can't be alpha."

"If Marcus keeps up his drinking and smoking, he'll kick the bucket sooner rather than later, and I'll take over," Shawn said. "I'll be free to bring you and your father back into the pack and name my own successor. And I would really like that to be you, Lucas."

He would've been lying if he said he didn't feel an instinctual pull to return to his pack. It was his family, his lineage. Werewolves had a lot of instincts that ruled their behavior. Belonging to the pack was one of them. He'd spent his whole life feeling like a guest in the place he called home, but it was still his home.

His place was with the Harts.

With Rosie.

FOURTEEN

ROSIE

FASHION DIDN'T COME EASY TO ROSIE. IT WAS ONE OF the side effects of living in a house full of men. *She* thought she had nice clothes, but she knew her attire didn't match what the other girls at school wore. Martha was no help, stalking around in something akin to a muumuu most of the time. Most days, Rosie wore a pair of jeans and a T-shirt—classic, basic. In the frigid winter months, she added a hoodie or a sweater. Nothing was better than the feel of an oversized sweater on a cold day. During the hot summer months, shorts and a T-shirt or tank top were typical—timeless and easy.

Rosie growled under her breath as she went through her closet for the tenth time in the last hour. Trying to find something to wear to the party had her stumped. She glanced at the clock, noting she had about a half hour before her father dropped her off at Becca's house. She planned to get a ride to the party with Becca after hanging out at her place for a bit. Sam was using the Explorer for his date, but he'd agreed to drop Lucas off at the party and drive them both home later.

Finally making a decision, she chose a plain black spaghetti-strap dress that hung to just above her knees. She put some mousse in her hair to make the curls look fluffy and soft as they hung over her shoulders and draped down her back. After dabbing on a little perfume, she selected a gold bracelet and necklace. Checking herself over in the mirror, she realized the dress was short enough to show the wound on her leg. Sighing, she rummaged around in her dresser until she found a pair of black tights to wear underneath. She had just shimmied herself into them when she heard a soft knock on her door. Assuming it was her father, Rosie called to him to come in. The door opened, and she turned to see Lucas staring at her.

His brown hair hung loosely on top of his head, like he'd run his hands through it, not bothering with a comb, and called it good enough. That was just his way, but she loved that about him. Her heart swelled, and she had a sudden urge to forget the party and stay home and watch a movie with him. His lips parted slightly, and a desire ran through her that felt right and wrong all at once. She shook her head. *Stop it. It's Lucas.*

She averted her stare nervously. "I thought you were my dad." Her stomach fluttered as she felt his stare linger for a few moments before he spoke.

"Um, I just wanted to catch you before you left. Sam said he's taking Heather to dinner and to text him when we're ready to leave the party..."

After he trailed off, Rosie nodded slowly. "Okay," she said. "That's cool with me if it works for you."

"Yeah... yeah..." Lucas trailed off again. He was still watching her, and a wave of self-conscious worry overcame her. Maybe she'd chosen the wrong outfit. Did she look ridiculous? "You look—"

Simon poked his head into her room. "Ready, Rosie?" He looked her up and down and raised an eyebrow. The self-conscious worry increased as she looked down at the dress and back up at him.

"What's wrong with it?" she asked helplessly. "Do I look stupid?"

Her father shook his head. "No, you look beautiful. But I feel compelled to not let you leave the house looking like that."

Cocking her head to the side, she fixed him with a disbelieving stare.

"Fine." He sighed.

"It's not that bad!" she said, raising her voice.

"Ah! Forget I said anything." He threw his hands up in surrender and laughed.

Lucas was edging toward the door, his face a mask of confusion and discomfort. Rosie grinned. She relished the softer side of her father so few had the pleasure to see.

THE RIDE to Becca's house was quiet except for a few exaggerated sighs from Simon. After the fourth or fifth sigh, Rosie finally huffed out a breath before she blurted, "Is something wrong, Dad?"

"I'm out of my element here, Rose." He sounded frustrated, which made her stomach flutter. Those who knew her best often flip-flopped between calling her Rose and Rosie, but the way he used her formal name now sounded serious. "I've had 'the talk' with your brother, but I never thought about needing to have it with you," he said.

"Oh God." She closed her eyes and wished for death.

"Please don't, Dad. Martha had the talk with me. You're off the hook."

He visibly relaxed as he muttered under his breath, "I love that woman."

Cheeks flame hot, she ground her teeth together. She really didn't want to be having this conversation. "You don't need to worry about that, Dad. I'm not doing anything."

"Good. That's good." He was quiet for a minute before he glanced her way. "You know to be careful if you do, right?"

"Of course."

"Because there are a whole world of implications if you have any...you know...kids."

Rosie studied the dashboard for a few moments and reached out to run her fingers over the textured carbon fiber trim before she spoke. "I thought the pack needed more members." Though it was the wrong thing to say, she was spurred forward by genuine curiosity. "I know I'm still too young, but we never talked about me having kids before."

"Rosie..." He sighed. "I'm not sure how that's going to play out. It might not be in the cards."

His words weren't all that surprising, but a part of her still died when he said them. Tears pricked her eyes, and she fought hard against them. Her life up until this point had been anything but normal, and something inside her cried out at the injustice of it. She always knew she would likely never get the white picket fence with a husband and two kids, but a part of her always held out some hope that maybe she was wrong.

"Damn. You know why, Rosie. I had to beg the Council to let you live. What would they do if you gave birth to more female werewolves? Or maybe the Council will want you to have kids, but what if your kids end up with witch powers like you?"

Rosie didn't trust her voice, so she just nodded.

He reached out and placed a hand on top of her head. "I love you, kid." The words came out in a whisper as he looked at her sadly. "You look so much like her, you know? You have her beautiful red hair and her cute little smile."

Rosie smiled through her tears. He didn't talk about her mother often, so most of what she knew, she'd learned from her grandma.

"Whenever I see you use magic…" His voice cracked, and he swallowed his emotion. "It astounds me every time, and it reminds me so much of her. I was amazed by everything she did. The way the flowers bloomed around her, and everything was always at peace in her presence…"

He took a deep breath and stared out his window, trying to compose himself. "I know you don't like to use magic. I know it makes you feel different. I haven't helped with that, and I'm sorry. But don't let that dim your light." He turned his gaze back to Rosie, making her heart skip a beat at the raw emotion in his eyes. "Of all the magical, wonderful things she created, you are by far the most amazing."

～

WHEN ROSIE GOT to Becca's house, her friend's nose scrunched like she smelled something bad, but Rosie knew it was her assessment of the black dress. Becca waited until Rosie's father was gone before she took Rosie's arm and pulled her into the house.

"That isn't what you're wearing," she said matter-of-factly.

"Ugh." Rosie threw her head back. "What's wrong with it?"

Despite her grumbling, she welcomed the distraction from the conversation with her father. A switch flipped, and she was no longer a female werewolf with freaky witch powers. She was just a teenage girl.

"If you want to turn Mason's head tonight, you need to do better than that number you got from the little girls' section at the department store."

"Huh?"

"You have to accentuate what you have," Becca said impatiently. "The booby gods haven't blessed you yet, but you've got abs that any woman would kill for, and even though they're sickly pale, your legs are sexy as hell."

Rosie stared at her. "Becca, there is nothing sexy about me."

"Not yet." She smiled mischievously as she reached into her closet and rummaged around.

"Nothing in that closet is going to fit me." She would kill for Becca's curves.

"Not my clothes, dear," she said with a laugh. "But my cousin is about your size, and I had a feeling we would be having this conversation, so..." She popped out of the closet, holding a green top and a short skirt. "Voila!"

"Wow," Rosie breathed. "That is a very short skirt."

"Put it on! Put it on!" Becca pushed the clothes at her. "The black tights look great," she said, eyeing up Rosie's legs. "They make your legs look so good."

After she changed, Rosie held her arms out to showcase the outfit then self-consciously wrapped her arms around her stomach. "Well?"

"Perfect!" Becca smiled.

Rosie turned to look at herself in the mirror. The skirt

hung low on her hips and fell to about halfway down her thighs. Becca was right—the tights made her legs look long and almost sexy. The shade of the green top looked just right with the color of her hair and was loose enough to hide what she lacked in the chest area. The cropped cut exposed the lower half of her stomach.

"Now, your makeup." Becca steered Rosie to her vanity and pushed her down into the chair.

As Becca rubbed eyeshadow over Rosie's eyelids, she prattled on about everyone in school. Rosie was only half listening until Becca started talking about Lucas and Sam. "Lucas has gotten hot as hell. The fact that he tries not to be makes him even hotter. He always wears those stupid shirts for bands no one has heard of. And would it kill him to run a comb through that hair every once in a while?"

Rosie frowned and fought the urge to speak up. Becca's words pissed her off more than they should have.

"And you know I've been drooling over your brother from day one. He gets dreamier by the day. I can't stand it. I would kill to live in that house with you. I would jump your brother's bones every day."

"Becca!" Rosie screamed, forgetting her anger. "Down, girl!" She felt her cheeks get hot as Becca cackled.

"Oh shoot," Becca said. "Don't make me laugh. I'm ruining your makeup."

By the time Becca finished, Rosie felt like a completely different person. Dark eyeshadow made her eyes smoky, and bright-red lipstick decorated her lips. Rosie started having second thoughts about going to the party, but Becca gushed about how beautiful she was. Rosie did feel more like the other girls at school. More than she ever had before. She kind of liked the feeling.

A voice in her head—a voice that sounded a lot like her

grandma—asked her why she was changing herself to be accepted, but she told the voice to shut up. For just once in her life, she didn't want to be the weird girl.

THE *THUMP-THUMP-THUMP* of bass vibrated the floorboards on the porch in front of Mason's house. When the front door opened, Rosie covered her ears at the loud blast of music. Conversation would be out of the question, which was more than okay since she was no good at making small talk. The noise also seemed to drown out her ability to read the emotions in the room. She'd been nervous about coming without her headphones, so the relief she felt at the distraction was immense.

It didn't take long for her and Becca to get separated. Rosie found herself wandering aimlessly and awkwardly not dancing while everyone around her bopped and weaved to the beat. She steered clear of the keg area. Her father would never let her out of the house again if he smelled beer on her. Her eyes tracked around the room as she fought the overwhelming feeling that she didn't belong. What made her think this was a good idea? Mason wouldn't want to talk to her. He could have any girl here. Why on earth would he want Rosie?

As her gaze wandered over the sea of kids, she locked eyes with Lucas. He was standing on the other side of the room with some of his friends. Something was different. After a moment, she realized he didn't recognize her. He was looking at her like she was a stranger. Suddenly, something in his blank stare shifted. His eyes widened, and he was across the room and in front of her in the blink of an eye.

"Rosie?" He had to shout to be heard over the music.

She smiled at him, but he didn't return the smile. He grabbed her wrist and pulled her through the throngs of people, pushing them aside mercilessly. He made his way into the kitchen, where the music wasn't quite as loud.

"W-what?" He looked her over, his eyes round. He'd seen Rosie naked dozens of times, but the way he looked at her now made her feel more self-conscious than she'd ever felt in her life. "That isn't what you were wearing when you left the house."

"Yeah," she said, pushing her hair behind one ear. "Becca—"

"Rebecca." Lucas threw up his arms and rolled his eyes. "Of course."

"What?" Rosie dropped her hand to her side, offended by his reaction. Becca was her friend.

"Nothing," Lucas said. "I think we should go."

Her jaw dropped. She wasn't prepared for that. A moment ago, her desire to leave had been overwhelming. Now that she was being told to leave, she wanted to stay. Because how dare he?

"I just got here, Lucas."

"Yeah, but..." He looked like he wasn't sure what to say.

"I'm not ready to leave yet." Rosie crossed her arms stubbornly. When he didn't say anything, she turned and stomped out of the kitchen. What was his problem? What gave him the right—

A tap on her shoulder startled her. Thinking it was Lucas, she spun, ready to tear him a new one. Surprise stole her breath when she found herself face-to-face with Mason. He flashed a bright smile, and her anger melted away. A flutter of excitement ran through her as his gaze focused on her. He mouthed something, but when Rosie couldn't make out what he was trying to say, she pointed to her ear and shrugged. He laughed and took a drink from his cup. Her stomach turned as she smelled beer. She shifted from one foot to the other and fidgeted awkwardly with her fingers, not sure what she should be doing. Scanning the room, she watched the people around her. Most were dancing and drinking, and some were trying to engage in some form of limited conversation over the music. Great. Dancing and talking—two things she sucked at doing.

Mason reached forward and ran a finger up her arm, eliciting a shy smile from Rosie. Goose bumps rose on her arms, and she looked into his eyes. Her smile faded. Something in his expression made her uneasy. His eyes were glazed, and he seemed a little unsteady as he moved closer. He set his cup on an end table and turned toward her, placing his hands on her hips. Slowly, he started moving them back and forth as he tried to get her to dance. It felt awkward, and she really wished he would stop. After a moment, he moved one of his hands up and ran it over the bare skin of her stomach. It tickled, and she tried not to flinch.

Mason clumsily reached for Rosie's hand then turned and pulled her through the crowd. Alarm bells rang in her head as they rounded a corner and went down a short hallway to a closed door. He opened it and pulled her inside, closing it behind them.

As Rosie's eyes drifted around the room, her stomach dropped to her knees, and she thought she might be sick.

Death. Everywhere.

Mason's family must have kept the local taxidermist in business. Mounted deer heads decorated every inch of wall space. Animal pelts were flung over quilt racks and laid out on the floor. Rosie's hand flew to her mouth when her attention zeroed in on one corner of the room where a wolf, stuffed and mounted to a pedestal, stared back at her.

"I said you look hot," Mason said, though the words came out in a slight slur.

"What?" Rosie turned and found him only inches away from her face.

"You look hot," he said again.

She winced at the stench of his breath.

His eyes wandered up and down her body appreciatively, and her apprehension grew. As she crossed her hands over the exposed skin of her stomach, she really wished she was wearing something different. Her gaze flicked back to the wolf, and Mason turned to follow her stare.

"Ah, you like it? My dad and I bagged that a couple a years ago. Gave us a run for the money, thas for sure." His face brightened, and his words slurred more with his excitement. "We musta chased her half the day, but we finally wore her down. Dad wants another. He started huntin' with this weird guy who told him about a wolf with a red pelt. They been out looking for it, and I get to go with 'em. Can't wait. Open season on wolves don't start till November, but they might open an off-season hunt soon."

Rosie's stomach dropped again. She remembered the terror of being hunted and closed her eyes, her heart hammering in her chest.

"I don't think we should be in here," Rosie said quickly.

"It's too loud out there. We can talk in here."

"I'm not very good at talking," she admitted.

"Well," he said as he took a step closer, "we don't have to talk."

Rosie took a step back and bumped into the wall. The

sound of distant music suddenly stopped, and someone started shouting. She turned her head toward the door, but Mason grabbed her chin and turned her head back toward him. He slowly slid his other hand into the waistband of her skirt.

"Mason—"

"Come on, Rosie. I see the way you look at me." Mason touched her hair, and Rosie turned her head away. She'd always dreamed of him touching her, but this felt awful.

"I don't look at you."

He laughed. "Sure, you don't."

His hand slowly trailed from her hair down her face to her collarbone. It rested there for a moment, and she felt a chunk of ice in her stomach as he slowly traced the hand down, down, over her chest.

"Don't," she said as she tried to push his hand away. Her voice shook, and she cursed her own weakness.

"Don't what?" he asked as he leaned forward and brushed his lips over hers. The light touch of his hand over her chest became harsher as he crushed her mouth with his in a rough kiss that tasted like beer and cigarettes. His hands were suddenly all over her, and she wanted him off.

This is wrong. This is wrong. This is wrong!

She let out a low growl as she pushed him away as hard as she could. Mason stumbled backward and crashed to the floor. Her body itched all over with the desire to shift, and she tried to control her breathing.

"What the hell?" he screamed. "You ugly-ass ginger whore!"

Rosie flinched, then faster than she could think, he jumped to his feet and was back on her. He shoved her against the wall and grabbed both of her arms, pinning them next to her so that she couldn't move.

"Let me go!"

Mason didn't answer. His brow furrowed angrily, and his glazed eyes grew stormy. His hands were back on her, roughly grabbing at her. She struggled against him, but he was too strong. She panicked as he reached for the hem of her skirt. Rosie screamed, and he quickly clamped a hand over her mouth.

"Shut up!" he growled.

She couldn't believe what was happening. Her heart thundered in her ears as she pushed as hard as she could against his chest, trying to get him off her.

In a whir of movement, Mason was suddenly pulled off her and shoved against the wall next to her. Rosie watched in shocked horror as Lucas smashed his right fist into Mason's face. Mason's head snapped back, and he slid toward the floor. Lucas grabbed him by the shirt and pinned him back up against the wall, throwing another punch to his face. Blood poured from Mason's nose as Lucas wound up for another punch, and panic gripped her.

"Lucas, no!" She grabbed his arm just as he was about to swing, and she held on with all her strength.

When he turned to face Rosie, she drew in a sharp breath at the murderous rage in his eyes. His glowing wolf eyes. He was moments away from changing.

"What the hell?" Mason cried, holding his nose.

Rosie ignored Mason and took Lucas's hands into her own. She closed her eyes to concentrate on sending a calming energy to him, but her own energy was too messed up. Her hands shook, and she cursed under her breath. When she opened her eyes, a tear slipped down her cheek. His face softened, and the glow faded from his eyes as he seemed to recognize what she was trying—and failing— to do.

He gently took her hand, leading her out of the room of death and through the crowd of people. All eyes were on them—or maybe that was her imagination. She tried not to make eye contact with anyone as he steered her toward the door. When they got outside, he grabbed her arm and turned her toward him. His eyes roamed over her body before he met her gaze.

"Are you okay?" he asked shakily. "Did he hurt you?"

She bit her lip. She wasn't okay. Mason had hurt her, but she couldn't tell Lucas that right now.

"I'm okay," she said with a voice that was steadier than she felt.

He nodded slightly and seemed to calm a little.

"We need to go." She started to walk away from the house and pulled out her phone, sending a quick text to Sam to let him know they were ready to leave.

As the adrenaline wore off, Rosie started to shake. What had just happened? What would've happened if Lucas hadn't shown up when he had? A dozen different emotions were at war in her head. She felt stupid for following Mason into that room. She felt weak for being so helpless. Mostly...she felt like a fool. She had such a crush on Mason, and she'd thought he really liked her.

And that room—all that death. The way he'd described hunting. Mason was a killer. And now they were hunting a red wolf...

A hand on her arm made her jump, and she looked up at Lucas.

"I wish I could calm you the way you calm Sam." His voice was soft as he watched her closely.

Should she tell Lucas about what Mason said? No. She couldn't. He would only worry and make her tell her father.

If she told her father, he would be furious. She would just have to stay out of the woods until it was safe.

Her mind went back to that room. To Mason's hands on her. The tears came, and she couldn't stop them. "I'm so stupid," she gasped.

Lucas pulled her in for a hug, and she melted into his arms. His embrace was firm but not crushing—safe, comfortable.

"You're not stupid, Rosie," he said.

"You tried to warn me," she mumbled as she pulled away from him. "You knew this would happen. You knew I was asking for it—"

"Hey!" Lucas almost shouted, and she jumped again. "I don't care what you're wearing. You didn't ask for that."

His eyes bored into hers, determined to make her believe him. Something in his stare penetrated her anxiety and put her at ease. Slowly, she nodded.

A slight smile touched his lips and he put a hand on her elbow. He looked at her the same way he had a dozen other times, but there was something in his eyes she'd never noticed before. A sincerity that dissolved her usual self-conscious desire to pull away.

"You're better than him, Rosie," he said softly. "He never deserved a minute of your time."

She wiped at her nose as he steered her to the edge of the street. They sat down on the curb, and she folded her arms over her knees and buried her face in them. His hand rubbed up and down her back, and she leaned into his touch, resting her head against his shoulder. His breath was hot against the top of her head, and she closed her eyes.

A few minutes later, a car pulled up to the curb, and Rosie listened as the door opened and a set of feet jumped out.

"What the hell happened?" Sam's voice sounded worried and angry as she looked up at him. She guessed her face was a mess of tear tracks and smeared makeup.

"Let's just go," Lucas said.

Rosie hesitantly stood up and followed them to the SUV. Sam opened the back door and watched wordlessly as she climbed in.

She tried to avoid eye contact with Sam as he watched her in the rearview mirror during the silent drive back to Hart House. The air in the SUV was thick with worry, and it made it harder to fight the tears coursing steadily down her cheeks.

When they got home, she ran straight to her room and ripped off her clothes. She put on a pair of yoga pants and a sweatshirt and wiped the makeup from her face. Her hands were still shaking, and her frustration mounted. She needed a run—badly.

A shudder ran through her as she remembered Mason's words about hunting the red wolf. She would stay close to the house where it was safe—it would be okay.

Rosie bolted down the stairs and ran straight to her father's office, barely noticing Sam and Lucas standing in the hallway.

"Is running still off limits?" she asked as she barged in.

Her father looked up at her, startled. "Rosie, are you okay?"

"I just really need to go for a run," she said impatiently. "Please."

"I haven't been able to find the hunter." He leaned back in his chair and watched her curiously. "Amos and I went out together to look. We found some ATV tracks and picked up on a scent, but we lost it by the ravine."

"Just for a little while," she begged.

"Rosie." Lucas's voice behind her made her jump. "It's not safe."

"Shut up, Lucas!" Shame coursed through her for yelling at him after what he'd done for her, but he was about to get them both into trouble. Sam stood off to one side, his eyebrows furrowed in confusion.

Simon stared at Rosie for a moment before he shifted his gaze to Lucas. "What happened?"

"We went for a run the other night," Lucas confessed. "I know we shouldn't have. We didn't get permission. But it was late, and we didn't think there would be any danger..."

"But there was," Simon said, his anger rising.

"There was," Lucas agreed. "There was a hunter. He shot at Rosie."

Rosie stared daggers at Lucas, but he wasn't looking at her.

Sam took a step forward, watching her. "Rosie?"

"I tried to draw the hunter's attention, but he wanted her. He had no interest in me," Lucas continued as he glanced at Rosie apologetically. "She was hit."

Her father's head snapped toward her so fast, she thought his neck would break.

"What? Rose?"

She sighed and rolled her eyes. "It's just a scratch."

"Let me see." His voice was calm but deadly.

Rosie lifted her pants leg up past her knee and showed him the wound. He rose from his chair and walked around his desk, squatting down to get a closer look. After he probed the area gently for a moment, he stood up and turned to stare out the window.

"There's more." Lucas whispered so low that Rosie almost didn't hear him. "Tonight, at the party, I smelled the hunter. There was some hunting gear laid out, and it smelled the same—"

"What?" Simon whirled around to face Lucas. "You know who did this?"

Rosie's stomach twisted. She hadn't picked up on the smell. Her senses weren't heightened the way Lucas's were.

"I mean..." Lucas's gaze flicked back and forth nervously between Simon and Rosie. "I think so. It was tobacco...and a cologne or aftershave. It was the same smell from that night." He looked at Rosie, his eyes pleading with her. "But I could be wrong. I mean, lots of people use the same kind of cologne."

"Who was it?" Simon pinned Lucas with a hard stare, making him shrink back. "I want a name, Lucas. Now."

"Mason Lewis. Or someone in his house at least. I didn't smell it on Mason. Just on the hunting gear."

Simon turned his steely gaze to Rosie. "You mean the Mason Lewis I told you to stay away from?"

Rosie dropped her head, a tear dripping down her cheek.

"He's dead," Sam seethed.

"No, Sam. Paul and I go way back. If he and his boy have been hunting our land, I need to handle this myself." Simon shifted his gaze to Rosie and set his jaw. "Pack your bags, Rose. You're going to your grandmother's first thing in the morning."

She turned her gaze to Lucas. He looked at her, shaking his head slightly.

"I'm sorry," he mouthed silently.

She looked away from him angrily.

"For how long?" she asked, her voice wavering.

"I don't know," her father said. "Until I decide it's safe. Clearly, I can't trust you to do what you're told."

"Daddy, I'm sorry!" Rosie cried. "Please."

"Go, Rose!" he shouted.

She jumped at his voice. He was angry...really angry. She stood silently for a few moments then took one last look at an apologetic Lucas and a shocked Sam as she rushed out of the room.

FIFTEEN
ROSIE

Driving up her grandma's driveway was like opening a fairy-tale book and stepping inside. Sitting on the outskirts of Hanks Hollow, Clara's cute little cottage was surrounded by aromatic flowering trees and bushes. A trellis laced with climbing blossoms framed the gated walkway to the front porch, where baskets of flowers perched along the railing. Behind the house, a stone walkway led to a sandy beach along Mingan Lake.

The car ride there had been completely silent. Simon wore a scowl and radiated anger as he kept his eyes fixed on the road. He hadn't spoken more than a few words to her since the night before. Rosie was furious with Lucas for telling her father about the hunter, and she was angry with her father for sending her away.

On the other hand, as Rosie approached the front door and melted into Clara's embrace, she realized a visit with her grandma might be just what she needed.

Clara was well known around Hanks Hollow as a healer. The gardens around her cottage were bursting with flowers and herbs she used to produce essential oils she sold to her clients, but what her clients didn't know was that the secret to her healing success was not in her oils. It was in her hands.

Between school and homework and life with the pack, Rosie didn't get the chance to visit with her grandma often, but when she did, she always learned more about herself and her magic.

"Oh, darling," Clara cooed as she held Rosie close. "You're so troubled, sweetheart. Come inside and tell me."

Clara was a walking contradiction. She had a tall, strong, solid build, and though she had a scrappy, no-nonsense vibe, her touch was gentle and soothing. She wielded gardening tools like a gladiator with a sword, but with those same strong arms, she wrapped Rosie in tight, squeezy hugs that she relished like a heavy blanket on a rainy day. Her long dark-gray hair had one large lock of white that cut through the gray like a river. Her green eyes were kind and frightening at the same time. She was the first to kiss Rosie's skinned knees, but she followed that up with a "suck it up" slap on the back.

A flowing dress fell to her ankles, and her bare feet were caked with mud. Some of her hair was tied atop her head, while the rest fell loosely around her shoulders. The only makeup that ever graced her weathered face was a dark shade of pink lipstick, and age spots dotted her tanned cheeks.

As Rosie unloaded the events of the past few days, she spared no details. She knew her grandma wouldn't judge, and she always had the best advice. Rosie needed that right now.

"Don't be so hard on Lucas, sweetie," Clara said as she patted Rosie's hand. "He cares for you so much. He doesn't want to see you hurt."

Rosie wasn't ready to hear her grandma's words of absolution.

"He got me in trouble!" she said as tears leaked from her eyes and wet her cheeks. "Dad is so mad at me."

"Ah ah," Clara tutted. "You got yourself in trouble, dear. Lucas did what you should have done in the first place."

Rosie crossed her arms and rolled her eyes.

Clara cocked her head and stared at her for a moment before she spoke. "How would you have felt if one of the boys went out for a run and got killed by a hunter?"

Clara's words hit home, and she knew it. Rosie couldn't say anything, so she just sighed and nodded.

"And we have some work to do, young lady," Clara scolded. "You should have felt Mason's ugly aura from a mile away."

"I know," Rosie said. "It's my fault—"

"That's not what I meant, and you know it," Clara scolded. "You can't control the actions of others, and you can't blame yourself when someone else tries to hurt you. That's on them, not on you." Her face softened, and she put a hand on Rosie's cheek. "But you should be more careful about who you choose to give your heart and your trust to, Rosie."

Rosie nodded and found herself needing to look away. Clara had a way of making her feel vulnerable. She could see Rosie—really see her.

"You have such a special gift, Rose." The hurt in Clara's voice was palpable. "If you would just choose to use it."

"I do use it, Grandma," Rosie assured her. "I've been working in the gardens with Daniel, and I've been using my energy to calm Sam almost daily—"

"But you can do so much more than that," she whispered. "You know you can. Are you still wearing those silly headphones? Take them off, Rosie. Take it all in. You'll never learn to use your gifts if you keep hiding from them."

Clara's face pinched in sympathy as a fresh round of tears welled in Rosie's eyes.

"I'm afraid to."

"Why?"

"So many reasons." Rosie laughed. "Don't I already have enough to deal with, being a wolf?"

"Why do you think these gifts are a burden?" That was the question. Her grandmother had asked it before.

"Because I'm an abomination."

That word—Amos had used it to describe her all those years ago, but she hadn't known what it meant at the time.

"Stop that! I don't want to hear that from you again!" Anger immediately reverberated from Clara. "Who told you that?"

No way was Rosie going to tell her about Amos. She never had and never would. If her grandma stormed Hart House looking to bust some heads, she would get hurt.

"I'm not afraid of those overgrown bundles of testosterone," Clara said as if reading her mind. She fixed Rosie with a hard stare. "Did your father call you that?"

"No! Never!" Panic raced through Rosie's veins.

Her father and her grandma seemed to get along, and she didn't want to ruin that. She needed them both.

Clara searched her face for a moment then sighed. "Well, whoever is giving you trouble is going to have me to deal with if he ever shows his face," she said. "We'll put this matter to bed for now, and I won't hear that word from you again. You are a gift from the gods, Rosie."

Rosie rolled her eyes, and Clara smacked her knee.

"Don't roll your eyes at me," she snapped. "It's true. Think about all the forces that were at work to bring your mother and your father together. Do you think that was coincidence? No, Rosie, that was the Goddess and the God finding a way to bring a little piece of their balance back to this earth."

"It doesn't matter," Rosie said. "Even if that was their plan, it will begin and end with me."

"What are you talking about?" The confusion on her grandma's face looked out of place. She had all the answers, always.

"I won't be allowed to 'mate,'" Rosie said, putting air quotes around the final word. "Dad said he had to talk the Council into letting me live. He doesn't know what they would do if I had a bunch of little female werewolf pups."

Anger oozed from her grandma though she hid it well from her face.

"That is not for them to decide," she snapped. "Who are they to think they can control what the gods have planned?"

Rosie didn't want to tell her that she didn't think the Council really cared about the gods. Stuart had told her they had old stories, but many werewolves seemed to think the gods were made up.

Clara made a disgusted sound and stood up. "No wonder you're so troubled, Rosie," she said. "You are surrounded all day by pompous men and their constant need for power and control. It's draining my positive energy just talking about it."

She moved to the kitchen and reached for a jar of purification incense. She hummed to herself as she lit the sage and let the purifying energy fill the room and rid it of the negative energy left there by their conversation.

"That's better," she said with a wink. "What do you say we have dinner on the beach tonight?"

OVER THE NEXT FEW DAYS, Clara guided Rosie toward a better energy. They spent hours on the beach, meditating under the sun with the soothing sound of the waves lulling them into a tranquil calm. Meditation on the beach had sounded ridiculous on the first day of Rosie's visit, but it quickly became one of her favorite parts of each day. The peaceful moments shared between them helped Rosie tap into the power and magic within herself.

They shared daily walks in the woods, where they breathed in the scent of the trees and observed the animals. Clara taught Rosie about the plants they found along the path. Rosie learned more about the local plant species in an hour-long hike with her grandma than she could learn in a lifetime on Google. Rosie's spirits lifted more each day. A peace came over her that she hadn't felt in a long time.

"You look better," Clara said as they walked through the garden one morning. "You're glowing again."

"Thank you," she said sincerely. Rosie didn't know what she would do without her grandma. Her presence in Rosie's life was a compass, always showing her the way.

"And you're looking better too." Clara addressed the potted moss rose plant that hung from a shepherd's hook at the corner of the garden as though it was an old friend. As her fingers traced over the succulent's branches, beautiful pink, yellow, and orange flowers blossomed under her fingertips. "You just needed a little more sun, didn't you?"

Clara looked at Rosie and smiled. There was a time that Rosie would have called her crazy for all the talking she did to the flowers, but she found herself doing the same thing with her plants from time to time, and she'd been talking to her old oak friend at Hart House for years. Clara would say that was progress. Of course, Rosie didn't let anyone but her grandma hear her doing it. The boys would never let her hear the end of it if they caught her.

"Do you feel them, Rosie?" she asked.

Rosie closed her eyes and took a deep breath. The air was light and happy. A floral mixture of a dozen different flower species tickled her nose. Their energies merged together just as their fragrances did. Picking them out individually was harder, just as picking out a specific smell from a mixture of scents could be hard. In wolf form, Rosie could separate and identify each individual scent. Clara was working with her to sharpen her magic so that she could do the same with her energy.

"Yes," Rosie said. "I can feel them."

Clara looked around, and her brow crinkled slightly as she looked at Rosie. A test was coming. "Are all of them happy?"

Rosie gave her a crooked smile and looked around. She let her hand hover over the plants and flowers as she walked, feeling their energy. It was positive and light... happy. She was about to tell her grandma all was well when her hand picked up a pinch of distress, just a tiny feeling that wasn't quite as peaceful as it had been a moment before. Rosie paused at a bleeding heart bush and knelt in front of it. It looked beautiful, its blooms forming lovely heart droplets and its leaves a rich green. But it wasn't happy.

"What's wrong?" Rose asked, touching the leaves lightly. Then she saw a thistle weed crowding the bleeding heart, making some of its blossoms wilt. "Is this guy bothering you?"

A small gardening spade appeared over Rosie's shoulder. She looked back to find her grandma beaming at her.

After taking the tool from Clara, she used it to dig the weed out by the roots.

"That's better." She inspected the bush closely and blinked. The branches were waving at her. She caught her grandma's grin as she glanced in her direction. "How do you do that? How do you make the plants move like that?"

"I don't make them move," Clara said as the branches bent and curled to her whim. "We share our energy and move together." Her gaze moved down to Rosie.

"You can do it too, Rosie," she said, "if you would just try."

Rosie stood up and looked at the bleeding heart. "How?"

"In a way, you do it already," she said, "when you help them grow. It's the same thing."

Rosie looked at her and scrunched her face. She didn't think she could do what her grandma was asking.

"Reach out and feel its energy," Clara said. "Focus on sharing your energy with it. Once you're one with the plants around you, you can use your shared energies to help them grow and to move together with you as one."

Closing her eyes, Rosie took in the energy from the plants around her. The moss rose, the bleeding heart, the shrubs, the roses, the peonies—she felt all of them, and she concentrated on giving them her energy. A rush of something powerful surged through her as she became one with them, and as the mix of energy inside her mingled together, it shot out through her pores.

Rosie opened her eyes, and all around her, fresh blossoms exploded in a variety of colors. She'd used her energy to help flowers grow before, but never like this. She looked at Clara, and her grandma smiled excitedly. Rosie raised her fingers and looked at the moss rose plant next to Clara. She concentrated on asking one of the branches to reach out and brush her grandma's arm, and she felt a tickle of excitement when it did.

~

DURING ROSIE'S STAY, Clara saw several clients. Rosie tried to keep out of the way, but she sensed Clara wanted her to watch, so she stayed close enough to listen. One of Clara's clients was a woman looking for a natural remedy for her backaches. The woman looked like she stepped off the cover of a Vogue magazine—definitely out of place in Clara's cluttered cottage. Judging by the size of the heels she strolled in on, Rosie suspected the source of her back problem was pretty obvious.

"I just can't handle it anymore. By the time I crawl into bed at night, my back is just killing me. My husband is getting frustrated because I never want to..." Her voice drifted off, and she glanced at Rosie. "Well...you know. Anyway. I heard you're good. I don't normally buy into the whole natural-remedy thing..." She paused and looked at Clara, seeming to gauge whether or not she'd inadvertently offended her.

"It's all right," Clara assured her. "Most people don't."

Clara had been holding the woman's hand the entire time. Rosie knew what she was doing. She could feel her grandma's healing energy from across the room. Clara finally stood and reached for a bottle on the shelf.

"First of all, you need to stop wearing those heels. They're ruining your back." Clara ignored the disgusted scowl the woman gave her. "I believe I have just the thing for you. Have your husband rub this on your shoulders and back every night," Clara said.

The woman took the bottle and inspected it closely.

"That's it?" she asked skeptically.

"That's it," Clara said.

A disappointed vibe lingered in the air around the woman as she looked at the bottle uncertainly. "What do I owe you?" she asked politely.

"This one's on the house," Clara said.

"Oh, thank you," the woman said, seeming relieved that all this visit had cost was her precious time. She stuck the bottle into her purse and made a quick exit, maneuvering her way unsteadily over the uneven stone walkway in her high heels.

"What was that?" Rosie asked after the woman got into her white Mercedes and drove away. "Will it do anything?"

"It's some jasmine, a natural aphrodisiac. It won't do anything for her back, but it will ramp up their sex drive," Clara said casually with a wink. "My energy can help with her back, but it sounded like she needed a little help in the bedroom too."

Rosie's cheeks grew hot, and her grandma laughed.

SIXTEEN
LUCAS

Streetlamps cast a yellow glow over the basketball court and lit the silhouettes of three young men as they played a game of Horse. The sound of the basketball hitting the pavement echoed through the night. Lucas watched from the passenger seat of the Explorer. The SUV was parked in the darkness of the street. His teeth clenched as memories of the night of the party ran through his mind. Mason's filthy hands pulling on Rosie's skirt, his hand over her mouth, the tears streaming down her cheeks as she fought him. He closed his eyes and took a deep breath.

"Seriously. How long are they going to play? We've been out here an hour." Sam's frustrated voice cut through Lucas's thoughts.

He opened his eyes and stared out the window again as Sam tapped impatiently on the steering wheel. Lucas sat up a little straighter as his sensitive ears picked up the sound of the boys talking. Sam could hear it, too, and they both stilled, listening to the faint sounds of the conversation.

"Come on, you guys! One more game!" Mason picked

up the basketball as it rolled across the pavement. "I'm not ready to go home yet."

"I'm beat, man. I'm out." One of Mason's friends, Chad, moved to the bench and picked up his discarded sweatshirt. "We did best two out of three, Mason. You got your butt kicked."

"Ha! He should be used to getting his butt kicked by now! How's that black eye? Beckett's got a wicked swing!" Mason's other friend, Jared, gave Mason a playful shove.

"What did you say?" Mason threw the basketball aside and shoved Jared. His friend stumbled backward but caught himself before he fell. "It's not my fault his freak girlfriend threw herself at me."

"Threw herself at you? That's not what I heard." Jared pushed Mason back.

"Yeah? Well, you heard wrong." Mason moved forward, shoving Jared again. "She wanted it. She wanted it bad. She would have gotten it if Beckett hadn't come sniffing around."

In the SUV, Lucas seethed. A low growl rumbled in his throat, and he reached for the door handle. Sam grabbed his shirt sleeve before he could move any farther.

"Cool it, Lucas." Sam's voice was low. "We need to wait. Chad and Jared both live up in the Liberty neighborhood. Mason's place is down on Elm. We'll get him when he heads home. He'll be alone then."

On the basketball court, Mason was still shoving Jared around.

"Cool it, Mason!" Chad moved between Mason and Jared. "It's late. Let's all just go home, okay? Just cool it."

"Whatever." Mason turned on his heel and picked up the basketball again. "I'm staying here. You pansies can go home and get your beauty sleep."

"Whatever, man." Jared spat into the grass before he and Chad wandered off toward the road.

Lucas and Sam watched Mason's friends walk slowly up the street. After their silhouettes disappeared over the hill, Lucas glanced at Sam and nodded. Sam nodded back, and they silently crawled out of the SUV.

Mason's head was down, concentrating on bouncing the basketball against the pavement. He didn't notice them until they were standing in front of him. As he glanced up at them, his eyes widened, and his mouth went slack as he dropped the ball. He turned his head toward the hill where his friends had disappeared moments before. When he turned back toward Sam and Lucas, his face was stricken in fear. Lucas gave a sly leer.

Words weren't necessary. Mason knew why they were there.

~

"Where are they?"

The sound of Simon's voice boomed outside the door of the small interrogation room, and Lucas flinched. Beside him, Sam sank down into the couch cushions. Interrogation rooms on television looked nothing like the small area where they were waiting. The two of them sat side by side on a small couch with a gaudy floral pattern. To the left was a small round table with two chairs. It reminded him of a break room.

The door was flung open, and Sheriff Craig Hill walked in. He was followed closely by Simon and Roger, both looking like they'd just rolled out of bed. Lucas winced. It was after midnight, and the late hour wouldn't win them any favor in the lecture they had coming.

Roger frowned as his gaze landed on the side of Lucas's face where a bruise blossomed and his lip was split. The metallic taste of blood lingered in his mouth. He'd been running his tongue over the cut for the past hour. Next to him, Sam had a brilliant black eye.

A heavy sigh came from Simon, and he placed his hands on his hips as his gaze wandered over them, assessing the damage. "Are you both okay?"

Sam's gaze flicked over to Lucas briefly before he answered, "We're fine."

"I'll leave you guys to it," the sheriff said with a small smile. "I need to go check on Mason."

Simon's eyes widened, and he fixed the two boys in the room with a hard glare as the sheriff closed the door behind him. "Mason? As in Mason Lewis? I told you to stay out of it. I'll take care of the hunters—"

"This had nothing to do with hunting," Sam snapped.

A heavy silence filled the room for a few moments before Simon squared his shoulders. "What. Happened." It wasn't a question. It was a demand for answers.

Lucas closed his eyes as Sam spoke. "He had it coming. He tried to force himself on Rosie."

After the sound of a chair scraping against the linoleum forced Lucas's eyes open, Simon seemed to stumble into the seat. The alpha's face paled, and his jaw went slack. "Rosie?"

"He tried." Sam's voice shook slightly. "Lucas stopped him."

A commotion in the hallway outside the room sliced through the thick silence hanging in the air. Voices carried into the room.

"Did you see my son? I want those boys arrested!"

Lucas didn't recognize the voice, but it was safe to assume it belonged to Paul Lewis.

"It was a fight, Paul. Mason is the captain of the football team. He gave as good as he got." The sheriff's voice was calm in the face of Paul's rage. "But if you want to press charges—"

The bang of the door hitting the wall made Lucas jump. He hadn't even seen Simon rise from his seat, but now the alpha stormed out into the hall like a bat out of hell.

"Paul Lewis, you keep that piece-of-crap son of yours away from my kids!" The walls practically shook at the decibel level of Simon's enraged yelling. "If I ever hear of him taking a breath within ten feet of Rosie, he'll have me to deal with. Do you hear?"

"Simon..." The sound of Paul's voice was no longer lethal. It was scared. "I didn't realize it was your boy Mason got into a fight with—"

"You bet your ass it was my boy. He was teaching your idiot son a lesson. And don't think I don't know you've been hunting on my land again. You're done in this town, Lewis. Finished."

Lucas had no doubts that, by the end of the week, Paul Lewis's name would be ruined with the town council, the local bank, and the Chamber of Commerce.

"Let's go!" Simon's voice boomed from the hallway, and Sam and Lucas leaped to their feet. They followed behind a silent Roger, filing out into the hallway.

Paul Lewis was standing in front of Simon. Eyes like saucers, he spluttered, "Simon, I don't know what you think Mason did, but—"

"Are we done here, Craig?" Simon shouted toward the sheriff, drowning out Paul's words.

The sheriff nodded silently, a small smile playing at his lips.

Simon stomped toward the doors of the police station, and Roger followed closely behind. Lucas took one final look at Paul, and his gaze landed behind the man, where Mason poked his head out of the other interrogation room, right next to the one they'd been waiting in moments ago.

He met Mason's eyes and smiled.

SEVENTEEN
ROSIE

On Thursday afternoon, Rosie sat on her bed, reading a book. Her grandma had a guest bedroom, but Rosie always thought of it as her own since she was the only one who ever stayed there. Clara was talking with a client, and Rosie had decided to use the opportunity to get a bit of alone time.

The call she'd received earlier that day from her father brought her the news she'd been waiting for. He'd decided that it was finally safe for Rosie to return, and he would come to get her Saturday morning so that she would be home for the Cramer pack's visit. It sucked that she still had to attend the party, but getting back to some form of normalcy was a relief.

Despite her excitement at going home, Rosie was really going to miss her grandma. The visit had been good, one of the best she'd ever had.

"Rosie, will you please give me a hand in here?"

At the sound of her grandma's voice, Rosie folded back the top corner of the page she was reading to mark her spot and headed toward the sound of her grandma's voice. As she came into the kitchen, her gaze landed on an older man sitting at the table. One of his pants legs was pulled up over his knee, which looked painfully swollen.

"Rosie, will you please rub this oil on Mr. Thompson's knee?" Clara gave Rosie a slight wink. "My arthritis is acting up again."

Rosie took the ointment from her grandma hesitantly. Clara had never asked her to help with a client before, and she wasn't sure how she felt about it. She stared at the nondescript jar of ointment and knew that, whatever it was, even though it had some homeopathic use, the real healing came from her grandma's fingers. Clara wanted Rosie to heal the man. A nervous flutter filled her stomach as she looked at her grandma helplessly. Clara gave Rosie a small nod of encouragement.

Rosie moved to the man's side and knelt in front of him. "Hi, Mr. Thompson."

A warm smile lit his face. "Thank you for your help," he said, pain evident in the waver of his voice.

Suddenly, his pain hit her like a brick to the face, and the intensity overwhelmed her. This poor man. As she reached toward his knee, the painful energy intensified. The healing warmth overcame her, bringing back memories of the day she'd healed Lucas so many years ago.

"The ointment, dear," Clara called out before Rosie touched the man's knee.

Rosie looked at Clara, and her grandma nodded toward the ointment in Rosie's other hand. Of course Mr. Thompson would think it was odd if his knee felt better from Rosie's touch alone, without the help of the ointment. Rosie rubbed it over her hands and massaged it gently into his knee. Warmth ran through her hands and out her fingertips as her energy passed to him.

Mr. Thompson gasped. "Good Lord," he whispered. "That's amazing!"

The swelling disappeared from his knee, and Rosie could no longer sense the pain.

"I've had this pain for years." He stretched his leg out experimentally and bent it a few times. He was silent for a moment, and when he tried to speak again, his voice broke, and he covered his mouth with his hands. "I couldn't even dance with my daughter at her wedding."

"I'm glad we could help, Mr. Thompson." Clara helped him up from the chair.

Rosie remained on the floor, her mind foggy and overwhelmed. She held onto the tears in her eyes, trying not to let them fall. His pain, both physical and emotional, had been indescribable.

Rosie could distantly hear them talking as her grandma led him through the house. She heard the closing door and her grandma's soft footsteps as she came back. Clara placed a hand on Rosie's shoulder and squeezed.

"That's why I do this, Rosie."

EACH EVENING over the course of her stay, Rosie and her grandma sat out on the beach to watch the sun set. Pinks and purples swirled across the sky, and the lake breeze was cool and soothing against her cheeks. It was the perfect way to end the day, and Rosie could see why her grandma loved it there.

"You did great this visit," Clara said to Rosie as they sat out on the beach on the last night of Rosie's stay. "You made so much progress. I'm happy you're opening yourself up to your potential."

A sense of pride warmed her cheeks, and Rosie smiled at her grandma. "It's hard," Rosie said honestly. "This life is so much different from my life as a werewolf. It's like night and day. Here, we bring life to everything. We heal, we help grow, we share energies and feelings. Werewolves are all about rules and territories and hunting and men."

Clara cast her gaze out over the lake and took a deep breath. "I'm going to tell you what my mother told me and what her mother told her."

Rosie studied her grandma. Clara's voice had taken on a different quality.

"Once upon a time, witches and werewolves lived in harmony," Clara said. "That's how the God and the Goddess intended it when they created the Chosen."

"The Chosen?" Rosie leaned toward her, willing her to continue.

"Most say our ancestors can be traced back to some-where in Europe. The God selected men from the earliest tribes and blessed them with the power to transform into the ultimate hunters. As wolves, the Chosen men could hear and see and smell better than any creature. They provided food and protection for their people.

"The Goddess picked women from the earliest tribes and blessed them with powerful energy that allowed them to commune and become one with the energy of everything around them. The Chosen women brought peace and healing to the people of the tribe, and they helped things grow.

"The Chosen men and women lived together in harmony, working together to protect each other and the life around them. Together, they created new generations of Chosen. The gifts given to the Chosen men carried down to their sons, and the gifts given to the Chosen women carried down to their daughters. Through many generations, they protected and provided for their tribes. Over time, their existence created legends, and the legends grew a life of their own. The Chosen men became known as werewolves, and the Chosen women became known as witches.

"Then things changed. The old ways of worshipping the God, the Goddess, and the spirits of the earth became sacrilege and were labeled witchcraft. The Chosen were afraid of persecution, and they went into hiding. Their history and true purpose, to protect and provide for their tribes, was lost.

"The werewolves abandoned the witches when the witch hunts were at their worst. They banded together in packs and became territorial, like traditional wolves. They started hunting and enslaving women to produce offspring and carry on their lineage and ensure their survival. They spread across Europe, Russia, and North America, staying in hiding and governing themselves."

"What happened to the witches?" Rosie wasn't sure if she believed what her grandma was telling her but realized, if it was true, it certainly explained a lot.

"The witch hunts took their toll. Chosen women hid, spread out, and became hard to find. Some witches joined covens and helped to spark the practice of organized witch-craft and magic. Some witches lived in solitude, and some tried to hide away their gifts and blend in with society."

Light from the fire danced across Clara's face as she turned to Rosie.

"Your gifts come from both sides, Rosie. That's never happened before. I won't pretend to know how hard that is, but what you are is special. If there is anyone in this world who can understand that balance best, it's you."

Rosie sat up most of the night, thinking about the conversation with her grandma. She watched through her bedroom window as the morning sun cast a glow over the lake, and she breathed in the smell of the water and fresh air. She would miss waking up to this. Living at Hart House was great, but she'd really grown to love her grandma's little cottage.

As she stretched the sleep kinks out of her back, there was a soft knock on the door.

"Come in," she said, a yawn slurring her words.

"Good morning, Rosie." Clara opened the door and poked her head in. "I know you aren't looking forward to that party tonight, but I have something for you."

Rosie sat up as her grandma moved into the room, carrying a garment bag.

"One of my clients is a seamstress, and I asked for her help."

Clara opened the bag and pulled out the most beautiful dress Rosie had ever laid eyes on. It was deep burgundy with a full, floor-length, flowing skirt. Embroidered vines bordered the neckline and skirt trim, and it had short, off-the-shoulder sleeves.

"Grandma," she breathed, "it's beautiful."

Her grandma beamed. "I'm really glad you like it." She took a jewelry box out of her pocket. "These will match it nicely."

Rosie looked at her curiously as she opened the box. Inside, a ruby necklace sparkled in the morning sunlight. A pair of matching ruby earrings sat on either side.

"Those are real," Clara said.

Rosie looked up at her, stunned.

"They belonged to my mother," she said. "Someday, you'll pass them along to your daughter."

Rosie frowned and tried to look away, but her grandma caught her chin.

"Don't ever let anyone, not even a council of were-wolves, tell you how you have to live your life."

"I wish it was that easy," Rosie said.

Clara opened her mouth to say something more but stopped herself, shaking her head almost imperceptibly. She held Rosie's hand. "Your father will be here soon."

As a rush of euphoria and calm swept over Rosie, she relished the feeling and closed her eyes. She realized after a moment that her grandma was using her energy on her, and she wondered if this was how Sam felt when she used her energy on him.

"I will miss you so much, Rosie," Clara said.

"I'll visit again soon, Grandma. I promise."

Her grandma smiled and gave Rosie's hand one last squeeze before she stood up.

"Get dressed," she called over her shoulder as she left the room. "You don't want to keep your father waiting."

After throwing on a pair of shorts and a T-shirt, Rosie put her hair up into a loose knot and walked out to the kitchen. She was about to grab a box of cereal from the pantry when she heard tires on Clara's gravel driveway and a short honk of a horn. She looked at her grandma, who was sitting at the kitchen table with a mug of tea.

"Go," Clara said. "You can have breakfast at home."

Rosie ran out the front door and leapt off the porch steps as her dad climbed out of the car. She flung herself into his arms, praying he would hug her back. She didn't feel anger from him like she felt a week ago, but that didn't mean it wasn't there.

As he squeezed her tightly to his chest, all Rosie could feel from him was love, and it filled her with joy. He kissed the top of her head.

"I missed you, kiddo," he said.

"I missed you too, Daddy."

"Clara." Simon nodded toward the front porch, where Clara stood, still holding her mug of tea.

"Simon." She nodded in return.

The exchange wasn't overly friendly, but it wasn't cold. That was how they were every time they saw each other. They didn't talk much, but their silence was amicable.

After they loaded all Rosie's things into the car, her father yanked playfully on one of her curls. "You ready to hit the road?"

Rosie moved to the porch, where her grandma stood, watching them. Clara's forehead creased, and she forced a smile as her eyes shimmered with tears. Watching her, Rosie almost didn't want to go home.

She reached up and gave her grandma one last hug. "Thank you, Grandma."

"I love you, Rosie. Remember who you are and what you're capable of. You're special. Don't forget that."

As the sun beat down through the windshield of the BMW, Rosie patted her hands absently against her pale knees and studied the freckles that dotted her thighs. She hummed softly to herself as she stared out the passenger window at the scenery. Snippets of the lake flashed through the trees as her father drove down the highway toward home. She hadn't left Clara's property once in the week she'd been there, and getting out felt good. Patting her knees again, she resumed a soft hum under her breath.

A hand on hers made her jump, and she stilled her movements as she looked at her father. As he gave her an apologetic smile, something flickered in his face. A strange, regretful sorrow, almost as if he was sorry he'd touched her. She wanted to tell him it was just a flinch, nothing more. He reached toward her once again, but this time, his hand extended past her to the glove compartment, and he pulled out her phone.

Forgetting the strange look he'd just given her, Rosie grabbed the phone from him and bounced happily up and down in her seat. Her grandma had a strict no-phone policy, so Rosie had to leave it behind for the week. She sighed in relief at the familiar weight in her hand. It was like a forgotten friend, and her mindless fidgeting stopped. She traced a finger over the passcode to unlock the device, and her eyes widened at the little text icon letting her know she'd missed thirty-eight messages. She guessed most of them were from Becca. They had an ongoing daily text conversation, and she hadn't had the chance to let her friend know she would be off the grid for a while. As she scanned the messages, her brows shot up.

BECCA: *Rosie! What happened?? Are you okay?*

BECCA: *Someone said you left. Did you get home okay?*

BECCA: *What happened?!?!*

BECCA: *I haven't heard from you, so I'm hoping you're okay. Text me!*

BECCA: *Mason is telling everyone you threw yourself at him Friday night. He's such an ass.*

BECCA: *What happened? Are you okay?*

BECCA: *Rosie!!!! WTH?!?! Sam and Lucas got in a fight with Mason. I heard the police were involved. What's going on?!?!?!*

"Dad?" Rosie's voice was laced with panic. "What happened—"

"You missed an...*interesting* week, Rosie," Simon said as he glanced in her direction. His gaze dropped down to her phone briefly before flicking back to the road. "Why didn't you tell me that little scumbag decided it was okay to put his hands on you?"

"Oh my God." Rosie buried her head in her hands and

sank down into the seat. "I'm just going to go ahead and die of embarrassment now."

"That's not funny, Rosie," he said angrily. "If someone hurts you, you tell me immediately. Do not make me hear about it through your brother and Lucas." He glanced Rosie's way, his expression softening. "And you have no reason to be embarrassed."

"I can't believe they told you about it."

"They didn't really have a choice when they got arrested for fighting with Mason."

"What?" Rosie's stomach dropped to her feet as she sat up. She stared at her father, but he didn't take his eyes off the road.

"They decided to take matters into their own hands instead of coming to me."

"Oh my God! Are they okay? Why would they do that?"

Simon finally looked at Rosie, his eyes burning with anger. "What do you mean, 'Why would they do that?'" His face contorted in a scowl, and his voice rose in frustration. "Why do you think, Rosie?"

"It was nothing." Rosie scowled and looked out the window. She couldn't meet his eyes. "I'm okay."

"Because Lucas showed up!" her father yelled. "What would have happened if he hadn't?"

She closed her eyes, not wanting to go down that road in her mind again.

The car suddenly pulled over to the side of the road, and Rosie's body jerked forward at the abrupt stop. Her hand shot up to the dashboard to steady herself as she turned to look at her father. She was surprised by his white-knuckle grip on the steering wheel as he stared straight ahead. Anger emanated from him, and she shrank into her seat again. Anger meant disappointment. The idea that she was the reason for his anger and disappointment hung heavily over her like a dark storm cloud.

"I'm sorry," Rosie said. "I shouldn't have—"

"It isn't your fault," he interrupted, voice firm. "It was that little scumbag. I knew it. I knew he would be just like his father. A vile piece of..." He took a deep breath then looked at her. "You know those boys would do anything for you, Rosie," he said. "And so would I."

"But beating Mason up?" Rosie didn't know if she should be angry, grateful, or scared. She decided she was feeling all three. "Like a couple of Neanderthals?"

"That was dumb," her father said, nodding. "But it came from a good place, and I can't say I'm not glad they did it."

Rosie looked out the window again as tears filled her eyes. She took a deep, shaky breath, and her voice wavered. "Are they okay?"

"They're fine," he answered quietly, still staring ahead as he pulled the car back onto the road. A small smile crept across his face. "I had a talk with Mason's father. I've been dying to let that dirtbag have it, and it felt pretty good to lay into him."

They approached Hart House, and Simon hit the remote control that opened the gate. He steered the car up the paved, tree-lined driveway, and Rosie felt a tremendous wave of insecurity as the house came into view. The whole pack knew about everything that had happened, no doubt, and she wondered if they would treat her differently. She'd always been treated with kid gloves, being the only girl, but this was different. This was girl drama in a house full of men. It would be tense and weird. She suddenly wanted to go back to her grandma's house.

Simon parked in front of the sidewalk leading to the front porch. Rosie stared up at the house as he climbed out of the car, and her pulse quickened.

"Daylight's wasting, Rosie," her father called.

The car shifted as he pulled her luggage out of the trunk, and she heard and felt the loud *thunk* as he closed it.

With a deep breath, Rosie opened the door and climbed out, dragging her heavy feet up the front steps toward the door. She followed her father into the house and was immediately tackled in a giant, Michael-sized bear hug.

"Rosie!" Michael lifted her up and spun her around. "It's been boring as hell around here without you, girly."

After he put her back down on the ground, Daniel took his turn.

"The flowers are wilting without you, Rosie," he whispered into her ear as he gave her a tight hug.

Stuart and Roger stood behind Daniel, each offering a smile and a nod.

"We missed you," Stuart said as he stepped forward. He hesitated for a moment before squeezing her hand. She forced a smile in return.

Rosie wasn't surprised to find Amos wasn't around, and she didn't mind at all.

A loud rumbling made Rosie jump, and she turned to see Sam and Lucas descending the stairs, shoving each other and stumbling along the way. They sounded like an elephant stampede. Sam leapt over the last four stairs and landed in front of her, his shoes slapping against the marble floor. She had a fraction of a second to get a glimpse of his black eye before he wrapped her in a tight hug.

"About freaking time you got home," he said.

She wrapped her arms around his waist, squeezing him tightly.

They all greeted her as though she had been gone a month instead of a week, but she didn't mind one bit. She was feeling loved.

After Sam released her, she glanced over at Lucas. A bruise decorated his cheek next to a cut lip. He stared at the floor, his hands in his pockets and his shoulders tight. Rosie remembered how angry she'd been with him when she last saw him, and guilt gnawed at her.

"You two are idiots," she scolded. Lucas's head snapped up to her, a crestfallen look on his face, while Sam looked like a deer in headlights. "But thank you. I love you too."

Lucas grinned, the tense lines of worry leaving his face.

"So, I guess you heard—" Sam started, but Simon cut him off.

"Let's just let Rosie get settled."

Rosie sighed gratefully. The last thing she wanted was to have a repeat of the conversation she'd just had with her father in the car.

As she headed to her room to unpack, her phone vibrated in her pocket. She took it out and glanced at it, not surprised to see another message from Becca.

BECCA: *I finally talked to Sam yesterday. He said you were at your grandma's and will be home today. Text me!*

Rosie sent Becca a quick message to let her know she was home and doing fine and promised to make plans to catch up with her. She opened the door to her room, and the familiar, inviting smell of lavender incense hit her. After skipping across the floor to the French doors leading to the balcony, she opened them, letting a warm breeze rush in. She threw herself onto her bed and sighed in relief. She was home.

~

By the time Rosie unpacked, her stomach was aching with hunger, and she remembered she hadn't eaten any breakfast. As if on cue, someone knocked on the door before it opened, and Martha barged in to gather Rosie in a big hug.

"It's good to have you back," Martha said as she squeezed Rosie to her large chest. Martha's hugs were squishy, and Rosie loved them. "I missed you."

"I missed you too," Rosie said, hugging her back. After pulling away, she grinned at Martha and led her toward the closet. "I have to show you what my grandmother gave me!"

Rosie carefully removed the dress from the garment bag, and Martha gasped.

"Oh, Rosie," she breathed. "It's so pretty."

"That's not all." Rosie took out the jewelry box and showed Martha the rubies.

Martha put a hand to her chest as she gasped.

"I'll do your hair up pretty," she said as she smoothed some stray hairs away from Rosie's face. "Oh, I can't wait to see you all dressed up!"

Rosie grinned as her cheeks warmed.

"Everyone has eaten already, but I saved some lunch for you in the kitchen," Martha said as she tucked the dress back into the garment bag. "I'll be back this afternoon to help you get ready." She gave Rosie a peck on the cheek and left the room.

~

After a quick lunch by herself on the patio, Rosie decided to wander through the garden to see how the flowers were doing. Just as Daniel had said, most of them were wilting.

"That won't do," Rosie said, running her fingers over them. Her touch perked them up. "I guess you guys missed me too, huh?"

She closed her eyes and reached out with her energy, just as she'd done at her grandma's, and she felt the flowers flourishing around her. The sharing of energy was intoxicating, and she felt dizzy with it. After a few moments, she opened her eyes and took in her surroundings. The bushes were blooming with fresh new blossoms, and their fragrance danced in the air. She took a deep breath and sighed happily.

"That's incredible."

Rosie turned at the sound of Lucas's voice and smiled. "I picked up a few new tricks this week."

"I guess so," he said, his gaze moving around the garden.

Rosie lifted a hand and gave a little wave. Lucas gave her a funny look and raised a hand as though he was about to wave back, but then some of the branches from the rose bush bent toward him and brushed against his arm. He jumped back with a screech, and Rosie giggled.

"You did that?"

She smiled shyly.

"It's really good to have you back."

"It's good to be back," she said, staring at the ground for a moment. "Thank you for what you did."

He took a deep breath. "I'll always have your back, Rosie."

"I know." She nodded with a smile. "You and Sam have always been there for me."

Lucas crinkled his brow as though he wanted to say more. When he didn't, Rosie sighed.

"I'm going to go for a walk in the woods," she said, pointing behind her. "I really missed it out there."

"You aren't going for a run, are you?" Lucas asked, looking unsure.

"No. I haven't fully recovered from the last slap on the wrist I got for going against orders. I just want to..." Rosie hesitated. She still felt funny talking about her magic in front of others. Even Lucas.

"You want to go and say hello to your tree and all your little forest friends." Laugh lines wrinkled around his eyes.

She wasn't annoyed by his teasing. Something affectionate in his tone touched her. "I would invite you to join me, but they don't really like strangers, so..."

"Got it," he said with an amused grin.

He put his hands in his pockets and turned toward the house. After a few steps, he paused and took one more look at Rosie over his shoulder and smiled again. She didn't know how she could've been so angry with him before.

Rosie turned and headed toward the forest, appreciating the feel of grass under her bare feet. The oak was up ahead, its branches towering high above the other trees, and she fought an urge to run to it. As she approached, she reached out a hand and placed it gently on the rough bark as she closed her eyes. The strong hum of its energy touched her immediately, and she sensed it missed her as much as she missed it. A light touch tickled her cheek, and she jumped in surprise. She opened her eyes and looked up to see that the branches were delicately reaching out toward her. Taking a step back, she reached her hands up to touch them.

Behind her, the familiar chirping of her squirrels caught her attention. She turned, and her eyes rounded at the sight of her little friends lined up at the base of the oak, watching her intently. Though they'd always been comfortable in her presence, they'd never actually paid attention to her like this before. Slowly, realization tingled through her. Something had been awoken inside her. She could feel the plants and animals around her like she never had before.

Her magic was growing.

"I swear to you, Rosie." Martha gasped as she wrapped a strand of Rosie's hair around the hot curling iron. Steam rose from Rosie's hair as Martha kept one hand on the curling iron and placed the other over her chest and rolled her eyes up to the ceiling. "That woman is cheating on her husband. I've seen a strange car in her driveway at least three times in the last month on my way to the grocery store. I'm telling you she doesn't deserve that husband of hers. That man works way too hard to keep that ungrateful woman happy."

Martha was a talker, and Rosie loved that about her. It took the pressure off Rosie to hold up her end of the conversation, something she'd never been good at doing. As Martha twisted pieces of Rosie's hair up and pinned them into place with bobby pins, a steady stream of gossip spilled from her mouth. Sometimes, Rosie wondered if Martha and Becca were related.

"There we go," Martha said with a proud smile. "Still got it."

Martha picked up the hairspray and pumped a sticky

cloud over Rosie's head. Rosie suppressed the urge to cough, and when the cloud cleared, she smiled at the finished style. Large, perfect curls were neatly piled on top of her head. A few of the curls spilled softly down the side of her face and down her back.

"Okay, little miss," Martha said, holding the dress out. "Hop in."

Stepping carefully into the burgundy pile of satin and chiffon, Rosie pulled the sleeves up over her arms. The dress hugged Rosie's body like a glove. She picked up the ruby earrings and fastened them in her ears as Martha draped the necklace around her neck. When she turned toward the mirror, her breath caught in her throat.

Vanity wasn't one of Rosie's vices. She avoided mirrors like they might burn her, but as she looked at herself at that moment, she found she couldn't look away. Under the soft tousle of curls atop her head, Rosie's brown eyes and full lips were accentuated perfectly by a modest amount of eyeshadow, mascara, and a deep shade of reddish lipstick. The sweetheart neckline of the burgundy dress sparkled with intricate sequined detail. The rubies framed her face in twinkling red. She looked elegant, a word she would never dream of using to describe herself under normal circumstances.

"A little step up from the T-shirt and jeans," Martha said, watching Rosie in the mirror. She winked and gathered up her things.

"Thank you so much, Martha." Tears misted Rosie's eyes, and she worried about ruining her makeup.

"Do you know how many times I wanted to dress you up over the years?" Martha asked, one hand on a hip. "You would never let me. You're a beautiful girl, Rose, whether you want to believe it or not."

A shy smile tugged at Rosie's mouth as Martha patted her shoulder before walking slowly out the door. Taking a deep breath, Rosie took one last look at herself in the mirror before turning toward the shoes Martha had left next to the bed. A curse spilled from her mouth when she spotted the heels. After sliding them on, she wobbled a bit before she found her balance and made her way to the stairs.

She was careful as she descended, taking one step at a time, afraid she would trip and fall. She was so focused on maneuvering down the steps that she didn't notice Lucas standing in the foyer until he spoke up.

"Wow."

Rosie looked up quickly, lost her balance, and squealed as she started to stumble down the last three steps. Lucas was quick to jump forward and catch her. So much for a graceful entrance.

"Sorry," Rosie said awkwardly, her cheeks hot. "I, um...tripped."

"I can see that," he said, smiling. "Are you okay?"

"Yeah," she mumbled, trying to hide her embarrassment. "Peachy."

Lucas's long, shaggy locks were neatly combed, and a tailored black suit had replaced his usual faded jeans and band T-shirt. The fresh smell of aftershave and cologne clung to him, and Rosie fought the urge to press her nose to his shoulder and breathe in the scent. She met his gaze and got lost in the ocean-blue depths of his eyes. His forehead creased, and he took a breath, like he was about to say something important.

"Holy crap!" Sam's voice made Rosie jump. "Look at you!"

"Thanks, Sammy," Rosie said as she turned to look at

him. That was probably the closest thing to a compliment she would ever get from him.

Simon, Roger, Daniel, Amos, and Stuart entered the foyer from the living room, where they must have been waiting. They looked like a handsome bunch, all dressed in formal suits.

"You look beautiful, Rose," her father said as he kissed her forehead.

Beyond the foyer and the stairs, the dining room was decorated with an array of flowers freshly picked from the garden. The large formal dining table was set with a white satin tablecloth and delicate dinnerware adorned with intricate floral patterns.

From the dining room, a set of French doors opened to the enormous stone patio, where an assortment of lounge chairs surrounded a large stone firepit. A patio table and chairs sat to one side, where the pack often shared meals when the weather was right. Out in the yard, twinkling lights accentuated the hedges and garden like magic.

The Cramers arrived in a large pearl-white Escalade that reflected the glow of the path lights lining the driveway. As they rolled up to the front of the house, the pack stood outside to greet them. Rosie watched as William Cramer climbed out of the car, followed by the remaining members of his pack. A young man, presumably his son, walked behind him. His blond hair was short and combed neatly to one side, and he had the greenest eyes she'd ever seen.

Two other men followed. One was short and muscular, with dark hair and blue eyes. He wore a scowl on his face and walked with a tough-guy swagger. The other man was tall and lanky. His brown hair was neatly combed, but his skin had a yellowish tint, and large bags hung under his eyes. He looked uncomfortable in the suit he wore, walking stiffly and pulling at his tie.

Rosie studied the two men and wondered which was Bruce. She'd never met the Cramer pack members in person before. She glanced toward Daniel and watched him eye the short, muscular man closely. Daniel's jaw muscles twitched like he was clenching his teeth, and his brown eyes were stormy. She had her answer.

She moved to Daniel's side and put a hand on his arm, sending a calming energy into him. At first, he looked like he was going to pull away, but then he relaxed and gave Rosie an appreciative grin.

As William and Simon talked, the young man's eyes roamed casually over the Hart pack. His eyes widened when they fell on Rosie. He held her gaze for a few moments before looking away quickly, staring at the ground in embarrassment.

Rosie continued to watch him for a moment before her eyes trailed back to William. With thick, wavy gray hair and wrinkled skin, he looked significantly older than Rosie's father. His posture belied his aging features as he stood with his back straight, exuding power. He addressed Simon and the rest of the Hart pack as he made introductions.

"My son, Calvin," he said as he gestured toward the young man standing next to him.

The young man's gaze met Rosie's again. She gave a faint smile, and he quickly turned his eyes down.

William pointed at the other two men. "My brother, Bruce, and my cousin, George. The youngest two members of our pack are still pups, and we left them at home."

Simon bowed his head slightly before introducing the Hart pack members one by one. All eyes were on Rosie throughout the introductions even when she wasn't the one being introduced. She self-consciously crossed her arms over herself as she felt the scrutiny of their stares. Sam and Lucas moved closer to her sides, and some of her anxiety melted away with their supportive presence.

"Remarkable," William said after introductions were completed. "I've heard of her...but to see her in person..."

He approached Rosie slowly and held out his hand. She glanced at her father hesitantly before reaching out her hand to shake his. Instead of shaking it, he lifted her hand up to his mouth and kissed the back of it. A warm flush spread across her cheeks, and he continued to hold her gaze as he addressed her father.

"Do you plan to have her produce offspring?"

"Jesus!" Sam shouted as Rosie's cheeks heated even more. "She's not a labradoodle."

"Samuel!" Simon admonished him sharply though his face was pinched in a disgusted scowl that told Rosie he wasn't particularly pleased with William's question either. "William is an alpha, and you will speak to him respectfully."

"It's all right," William said as he looked in Sam's direction. "He's right. My apologies, Miss Hart."

Rosie wasn't sure what to say, so she just nodded.

"I have spoken to the Council, and they are holding conference on the matter," Simon said, his eyes flicking briefly in Rosie's direction.

She tried not to gawk at him. She had no idea he'd spoken to the Council about it.

"Let's go inside," Simon continued. "I believe dinner will be ready shortly."

The unnerving stares didn't subside during dinner. Calvin didn't seem to have any shame in the way he watched her openly. It was only when she locked eyes with him that he looked away bashfully.

"Dude," Sam said after the fifth or sixth time he found him gaping at Rosie.

"Samuel!" Simon chided with an embarrassed sigh.

"You'll have to excuse Calvin," William said as his son looked down at his plate with scarlet cheeks. "He is home-schooled, so he rarely sees members of the opposite sex—and certainly never one so beautiful." He winked at Rosie, making her blush again.

As a low hum of laughter circulated the table, Bruce smacked the back of Calvin's head. "Get a grip, kid," he said with a grin before turning his stare back at Rosie, his grin fading.

Rosie fought an urge to tell Bruce he wasn't doing much better with the whole staring thing. Bruce's stares were vastly different from Calvin's. His angry energy felt similar to what she felt from Amos, and it gave her a sinking feeling.

Martha entered the room and moved around the table, clearing some of the dishes. William glanced her way for a moment, and his lip curled. "Really, Simon. I think it's time for you to trade your help in for a newer model. She's nothing to look at, that's for sure."

A jolt ran through Rosie's body, and she had to bite her lower lip to hold her scream. The scarlet coloring of Martha's cheeks was the only indication she'd heard the insult as she finished clearing the dishes and hurried out of the room.

"She's a person, not a car." Rosie's voice shook as she spoke.

William's eyes widened as his gaze flitted to her. Next to him, Simon glanced down at the table. His silence was deafening, and for the first time in her life, Rosie was ashamed of her father. Martha had been with their family for years, yet he sat there and said nothing while she was disrespected.

"She has a mouth on her, Simon." William held Rosie's gaze until she turned her eyes away, stinging with tears. "Have you thought about what you'll do with her?"

"What do you mean?" Simon glanced toward Rosie before he looked at William.

"Well..." William took notice of Simon's cold stare. "Surely you don't plan to keep her here. She needs to be bred, Simon. Think about it. We could have a whole new nation of pure werewolf blood. We wouldn't need humans mucking up our lineage anymore. Look at George over there." He gestured toward his nephew, whose pallid complexion was even more yellow under the light of the chandelier. "He inherited his alcoholism from the junkie woman my uncle knocked up. He's a disgrace to our heritage."

"You don't mean to create more female werewolves?" Amos's voice was full of disgust, and a sneer crossed his face. "That's absurd. This one was a mistake, and it should be the only one ever made."

"Amos!" Simon slammed a hand down on the table as he spoke, and the room fell silent.

Rosie's insides churned. She swallowed the bile rising in her throat and fought an urge to run from the room. Next to her, Lucas reached into her lap and took her hand, squeezing tightly.

"I will not hear any more of this talk tonight," Simon said quietly. "We are here to discuss the rogue, not my daughter."

William stared at Simon for almost a full minute before

he took a deep breath. "Of course. My apologies, Simon. Now about that rogue..." He glanced around the table, smiling. "I'm not trying to accuse you, but I'm telling you he smelled of this pack."

Amos spoke up. "That's not possible. We have all been here."

"I can't explain it," William said. "I'm just telling you what I know."

Simon glanced around the table then back at William. Rosie noticed that he avoided her gaze.

"Let's enjoy a little bit of fresh air before we take this discussion to my office," he said.

Rosie couldn't move fast enough as everyone rose from the table. She raced to the patio, gulping hungrily at the fresh air. She needed every ounce of her strength to keep the tears at bay. Moving to the railing, she stared out at the garden lights. While she concentrated on her breathing, Rosie finally heard Calvin speak for the first time.

"I'm sorry," he said. Rosie turned toward him, and Calvin smiled bashfully. "I didn't mean to be so rude, staring at you like that," he added. "It's just...you're so beautiful."

His forwardness caught her off guard, rendering her speechless. The surprise must have shown on her face because he quickly backtracked.

"I mean, maybe that wasn't the right thing to say." He sighed. "Can I start over?"

Rosie smiled tightly. His staring was the least of her worries. He was either pretending the conversation at dinner hadn't happened, or he truly had no idea how horrifying it was.

She shrugged, tears stinging her eyes. "Sure."

"Okay, cool," he said with a relieved smile. "I'm Calvin."

"I'm Rosie."

"I know." He chuckled. "Everyone knows who you are. My father talks about you all the time."

Rosie flinched.

Calvin's face blanched. "I didn't mean all the time. Just...never mind." He bit his lip and turned his face away as he shifted from one foot to the other.

The feeling of being watched tickled Rosie's senses again, and she looked toward the house. To her surprise, it wasn't the Cramers this time. Lucas watched their exchange closely, a strange expression on his face. A few feet away from him, Amos watched as well. She could feel his angry energy even from this far away, and Amos glared at her with a dark scowl.

"Rosie," Daniel called from behind her.

She turned to see him approaching slowly.

"It was really nice to meet you, Rosie," Calvin said, sparing a quick glance Daniel's way. He turned to make a hasty escape but took one last look at her over his shoulder. "Really."

Rosie crinkled her brow as she watched him walk away. He drifted off toward where Bruce and George sat on the other side of the patio and sat down, a frown etched on his face.

"I told you none of them want to be near me." A sly smile spread across Daniel's lips. "I'm sorry if you were enjoying that very awkward-looking conversation."

"Thank you, Danny." Rosie smiled, using the pet name he allowed only her to use. "My knight in shining armor."

"Dinner was weird, right?" he said, giving her a smirk. "Don't worry, okay? Your dad won't let anything bad happen to you. And forget Amos. You were never a mistake. Maybe you were a surprise, but you're the best surprise this pack has ever had."

Rosie felt her mood lightening and felt grateful, particularly because she knew this night had to be rough on Daniel. "How are you holding up?"

"I'm okay," he said, nodding casually. "I want to tear his throat out, but I've held off, so that's good."

"Your restraint is remarkable." Rosie laughed then looked toward the other end of the patio, where Stuart was standing by himself, seeming lost in thought. "How do you think Stuart is doing?"

"Grandpa holds the pack rules in high regard and won't do or say anything to stir things up," he said. "Besides, I don't think he really has feelings—just memories and stories."

Rosie considered telling him how wrong he was about Stuart. Her great uncle didn't show his feelings, but he felt them nonetheless. They'd all spent time listening to Stuart. While he didn't wear his emotions on his face as he spoke about pack history, pride poured from him. Sadness tainted his words when he spoke about members of the pack who had passed, and when he recalled stories from his younger years, she sensed an innocent joy and a feeling of longing. Rosie would bet that he often wished he could return to his youth. She would also bet that he harnessed as much hatred toward Bruce Cramer as Daniel did. Jack was Stuart's only son.

Her chest tightened. Her fond memories of him were tainted by what she'd learned of his past. What she wouldn't give to go back to knowing him as the sweet, innocent old Stuart she'd always loved.

THE EVENING WORE ON, and Rosie's boredom became almost unbearable. As future alphas, Sam and Calvin were both in Simon's office, observing and learning from the meeting with the current alphas. The remaining members of both packs lingered on the patio, and an awkward, tense silence hung in the air. Alcohol started flowing a little more freely among the elder members of both packs.

Rosie decided to take a walk to get away from the crowd. The gazebo and garden were in the far corner of the yard, and a maze of large, immaculately trimmed hedges surrounded it. The lights made it all look like something out of a fairytale. She was making her way through the hedges when she felt Amos approaching seconds before she smelled him. He'd been drinking heavily, and his energy was uninhibited and angry.

"Well, there she is," he said, slurring his words slightly. "Our little strumpet."

"What?" She wasn't sure what he was calling her, but she could guess it wasn't a term of endearment.

"I heard things didn't go so well with your little *crush*," he said, emphasizing the word with a snarl. "Mason, was it? Mason, Lucas, Calvin. My, my, you're really getting around, aren't you?"

A bubble of anger rose in her chest. He was calling her a slut.

He'd boxed her into a corner of tall hedges. She tried to maintain a wide berth as she walked away, but it wasn't wide enough. He grabbed her arm tightly and gave her a little shake.

"Where are you going?" he demanded. "I'm not done—"

"Amos." Lucas appeared seemingly from nowhere. "I think I heard Simon calling for you."

Amos let go of her with a jerk of his arm before giving Lucas a long, hard stare then stumbling away.

"Are you okay, Rosie?" he asked as they watched Amos clumsily make his way back to the house.

"I'm fine." Rosie rubbed at her arm where Amos had held her.

"Liar." Lucas frowned. "He was out of line, and he was wrong. You're not a strumpet."

"I don't even know what that means," she said, letting a tear fall. She wiped at it in frustration.

Lucas looked like he was mulling over how to explain it.

"I think I can guess," she said, rolling her eyes.

"It doesn't matter. He's drunk, and he's an ass."

"I barely said two words to Calvin. And you..."

"What about me?" He took a step toward her, watching her closely.

"You're my best friend."

"Is that all?" His eyes bored into hers intensely, the garden lights making them twinkle like gems. His brows knit together and he bit his lip.

Rosie didn't say anything, and he looked away briefly.

"You know, when you had a crush on Mason, I was insanely jealous."

"What?" Her insides twisted. She couldn't have heard him right.

He turned back toward her. "And tonight, when Calvin was talking to you, I wanted to punch him."

"That would have been highly unnecessary," she said as he took another step closer.

"I've been trying to be subtle, but you don't take subtlety well." Lucas reached up. His hand hesitated at the side of her face for only a moment before he brushed a strand of hair away from her face. "You look so beautiful tonight."

"Lucas?" Rosie wasn't sure what she was asking.

He leaned forward, his face inches from hers. "I think you feel it too," he whispered. "Am I wrong?"

Rosie shook her head, unable to speak, and he touched her cheek gently as his head dipped down and his lips met hers. A spark of joy and anticipation and longing ignited, and she realized she hadn't known how much she wanted him to kiss her until that moment. Her mind went blank, and all she could focus on was how much she wanted him there with her. He deepened the kiss slightly, and she parted her lips, inviting it. Her body hummed with electricity, and she reached up to touch his face. His kiss intensified as the current ran between them, exciting and warm. Something sparked inside her, like a match ripping against friction, and a flame roared to life. It burned warm—the most pleasant heat she'd ever felt in her life. After a minute, he pulled away, and she felt cold where his warmth had been a moment before.

Lucas looked at Rosie, his pupils blown, his cheeks slightly flushed.

Wow.

Rosie thought the word in her head, but she could've sworn she heard him echo it.

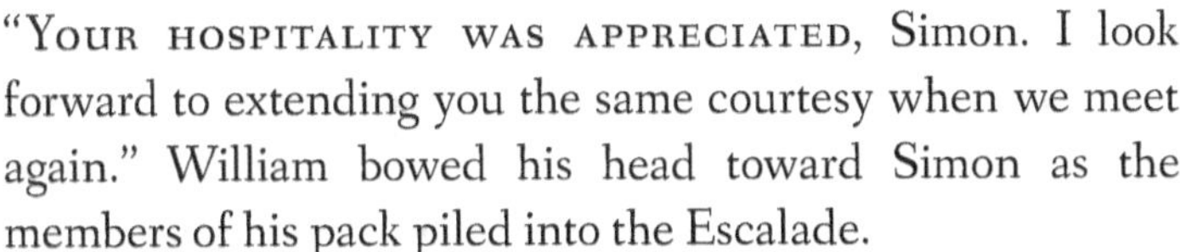

"Your hospitality was appreciated, Simon. I look forward to extending you the same courtesy when we meet again." William bowed his head toward Simon as the members of his pack piled into the Escalade.

Rosie groaned. She couldn't wait for them to leave.

After their kiss, she and Lucas had made their way back to the house just in time for the Cramers to announce their leave. Her gaze trailed over to Lucas. He was watching her, and her cheeks heated as she smiled at him.

"Miss Hart."

Rosie jumped, and her gaze swiveled back to William, who'd called out to her.

"It truly was a pleasure, and I hope that you will consider coming to visit us sometime. I know that Calvin would love the pleasure of your company."

A heavy chunk of ice settled in Rosie's stomach at the thought of being alone with the Cramer pack. There was nothing she could say. She couldn't even muster a smile.

"Thank you for the visit, William." Simon's voice pulled the focus off Rosie, and she was grateful. "As I said, you have our full cooperation. If the rogue comes into your territory again, we'll help you find whoever it is."

William nodded and glanced at Rosie one last time before getting into the giant SUV. The shiny white vehicle drove away, and Rosie let out a breath of relief. Silence hung heavily in the air for a moment before Simon cleared his throat.

"Michael will be here any moment. Then we'll go for a run." His gaze flicked to Rosie. "Rosie, come to my office. I want to talk to you."

Anger bubbled in Rosie's chest, but she stayed silent as she nodded and followed Simon into the house. As they moved into his office, he shut the door.

"Are you okay?" Simon didn't look at her as he asked.

Rosie crossed her arms over her chest. "I've been better." Her voice shook.

"I didn't want your first experience with other werewolves to be like that." He sighed. "But I guess I shouldn't be surprised. Things haven't changed."

"You owe Martha an apology." Rosie couldn't hide the anger from her voice. She would never dream of telling her father what to do, but she couldn't stand for what had happened.

"Martha has been in the werewolf world for a long time, Rosie. She's used to it."

Rosie's jaw dropped. "That doesn't make it right!"

"No, it doesn't." He lowered his head. "You're right. I'll talk to her."

She nodded and turned, but her father caught her arm.

"Rosie." He looked her in the face. "You were never an accident. You are a gift."

TWENTY

LUCAS

THE SONG OF HUNDREDS OF FROGS CHIRPING IN THE distance filled the darkness of the night as Lucas crept through the trees. He trailed behind the rest of the pack and watched as they all followed closely behind Simon. To anyone who happened across them, they looked like a typical pack of gray wolves.

Except for Rosie.

She glanced back at him briefly as she jogged along behind her father. Her fur was like fire, and the pop of red stuck out among the shades of gray on the other wolves. Tufts of white fur peppered her chest and belly, but the rest of her body was a brilliant scarlet. When the sun hit her in the daytime, she looked like a phoenix.

A sour taste lingered in Lucas's mouth from the Cramers' visit earlier that evening. He knew the werewolf world was full of jerks. He'd heard plenty of stories. Still, hearing the pompous, distasteful things that came out of William's mouth was surreal.

Worse still was watching Calvin cozy up to Rosie after

dinner. Jealousy tightened his chest. Rosie wasn't his, yet he felt a strong territorial hold over her. He'd never felt anything like it. He knew he needed to make his move. It was now or never. And God, he was so glad he did. That kiss was nothing short of amazing, and he couldn't wait to do it again.

He slowed his pace as Simon came to a halt at the head of the pack, nose to the ground as he picked up a scent. Lucas loved nights like these. The night air felt so much better when he took wolf form. He became one with the forest, and everything came alive.

A deafening snap echoed through the night, and hard-wired instinct spurred Lucas into motion before his brain comprehended what he was doing. He hunched into a defensive stance, curling his lips to display his teeth. A split second later, a cry of agony filled the air. Ahead of him, Michael, still in wolf form, lay on the ground, writhing in pain. Blood poured from a mangled leg trapped in the sharp steel jaws of a trap.

After a moment of shocked silence, the pack members jumped into action, rushing to Michael's side. Daniel was the first there, low whimpers of concern emanating from him as he nudged at the trap with his nose. Michael let out a sharp yelp of pain, and Daniel skittered backward.

"Everyone back up!" At Simon's telepathic order, the pack members made room for their alpha as he rushed to Michael's side and shifted to human form. He went to work on the trap, finding the release mechanism and pulling it away. He tossed it aside in disgust, and it clanged loudly as it hit the forest floor.

Blood was gushing from Michael's leg at an alarming rate, and Simon held his hands over the injuries, trying to stem the flow.

He spoke in a low, angry tone. "I think it hit his femoral artery."

One by one, the remaining pack members shifted to human form as they surrounded Michael, who let out a scream of pain as he shifted to human form himself. His lower leg was a mess of blood where deep puncture wounds had left gaping holes. Lucas thought he saw a flash of bone, and he closed his eyes as his stomach roiled.

Rosie was suddenly next to Lucas, reaching for his hand as her ragged breathing hitched. There was a faraway look in her eyes for a moment before she glanced around the circle of pack members. Her gaze landed on Amos, and her eyes flashed briefly in fear before her eyebrows furrowed in determination. She squeezed Lucas's hand before letting go and taking a step forward. Slowly, she knelt beside Michael and reached forward to place her hands gently on his leg.

It was instantaneous. One moment, Michael was bleeding out on the forest floor, and the next, his wounds were gone. Blood still coated his leg, but the puncture wounds were healed.

Michael's cries of pain died away, and his eyes were like saucers as he stared at her. "It doesn't hurt anymore. How did you—"

"It's witchcraft." The anger in Amos's voice made Rosie flinch.

"Shut up, Amos!" Simon's voice was lethal as he leaned forward and inspected Michael's leg.

Rosie seemed to shrink in on herself as she took in the stares from the pack. Her gaze landed on Lucas, and her arms shot to her chest, covering herself. Lucas's cheeks heated, and he was suddenly very aware that he was also naked. They were no strangers to nudity, but something in the way Rosie looked at him now had him shifting on his feet.

In a red streak of movement, Rosie shifted to wolf form and took off through the woods.

SUNDAY BRUNCH in all its glory was set out on the table. Eggs, French toast, pancakes, sausage, bacon, chicken, venison, ham, potatoes. Lucas could barely look at it. His stomach was full of butterflies. It was cliché, but it was the only way to describe the fluttering feeling that had taken hold.

Across the table, Rosie stared at her plate silently. She hadn't touched her food. Maybe she had butterflies too. He hoped she was thinking about their kiss like he was, but she was much more likely distracted by Amos, who was pinning her with a hard glare.

The usual mealtime competition to see who could talk the loudest had been replaced by a silence punctuated by the occasional clang of silverware. The events of the previous night hadn't been mentioned, but they were surely at the forefront of everyone's mind.

After shifting the food around on his plate for a few minutes, Lucas raised his eyes to look across the table at Rosie again. His cheeks heated when he met her gaze. She was watching him, a soft smile on her lips. Maybe she really was thinking about their kiss.

After brunch, Lucas sat out on the patio to read his book. It'd had him on the edge of his seat yesterday, but now he couldn't focus on the words. His mind kept drifting back to Rosie. He leaned back and propped his feet up on the chair next to him. They hadn't talked since their kiss. Should he go find her? What would he say?

"What are you reading?" Rosie's voice caught Lucas by surprise, and his legs dropped to the ground as he spun in his seat. "I'm sorry. I didn't mean to scare you."

It was one of the rare occasions she wore her hair down, and the soft curls spilled over her shoulders and down her back. The red color popped vibrantly against her yellow tank top and ivory skin. Her hands fidgeted nervously in front of her, and she pulled mindlessly at the hem of her shirt.

"Hey, Rosie." Lucas put his book down on the patio table and cleared his throat. "What are you doing?"

"I was going to go for a walk..." Her voice drifted off as she looked out toward the forest.

Rosie spent a lot of time in the woods. She sat at the large oak tree at the edge of the yard all the time. Sometimes, he would sit in the shade of the hedges nearby and watch her. She talked to herself a lot. Or maybe she talked to the tree. He wasn't sure.

"Didn't your dad say we weren't supposed to go out to the woods alone?" Lucas crinkled his brow in exaggerated disapproval.

"I'm pretty sure I'll be safe from wolf traps at the edge of the yard." Her eyes drifted back out to the forest, and she bit her lip. "But if you think maybe it's best I don't go alone, you could come with me." A hopeful smile tugged at her lips.

The butterflies reappeared in Lucas's stomach. He stood slowly and held out a hand. A bashful smile spread across her face as she ducked her head and placed her hand in his.

The walk was quiet until they reached the edge of the

yard. Rosie halted suddenly, her brow creased in concern as her eyes flitted over the garden in front of them. Lucas looked toward the garden, wondering what had her so concerned. The answer hit him then. The greenery was devoid of flowers, having been picked over the previous afternoon. Daniel had trimmed dozens of buds for Martha to arrange into decorative displays in the house.

"I just need to take care of this," she said softly.

Lucas stayed put as she made her way through the gate then paused for a moment before moving among the bushes. As she moved, new blossoms bloomed around her as though she was waking them from sleep. Reds and yellows and oranges popped, and soon the garden was alive with brilliant color. Breath caught in Lucas's throat as he watched her work. Her red hair glowed in the sun, and her beauty put the flowers around her to shame. She closed her eyes, and a peaceful smile graced her lips.

She stepped out of the garden, and as she approached him, her amazing magical presence turned timid and shy.

They made their way toward the woods, and Rosie stopped in front of her oak tree. The branches swayed toward her as she approached though no breeze was blowing. Blinking, Lucas stared at the tree, but Rosie didn't seem fazed by the phenomenon. She turned to look at him briefly before taking a seat on the ground.

A bolt of courage ran through him, and he sat on the ground next to her, close enough that their legs touched. He reached into her lap and took her hand, lacing his fingers between hers. Tingles ran through his hand—pleasant tingles, not the pinpricking kind.

After a moment of silence, Rosie looked into Lucas's face. "This is stupid. It shouldn't be so awkward. We've known each other forever. Why do I suddenly feel so shy around you?"

"Don't be shy, Rosie. Not with me."

Her face lit up as her lips curved into a smile. They were pink and looked incredibly soft. The urge to claim them overtook him, and he leaned forward, brushing his mouth over hers. An electric current hummed through his body. And that flame—the flame that had sparked the night before—roared to life inside him again.

"Mine." An unfamiliar territorial claim for her rang through his head. *"You're mine."*

"Yes. And you're mine."

The sweet telepathic voice in his head startled him, and he jerked back. Her eyes widened in shock as their gazes met. Wolf telepathy was only supposed to work in wolf form.

"Can you hear me, Rosie?"

"I can hear you, Lucas."

An irresistible urge ran through him, and Lucas lunged forward, taking her mouth with his. She kissed him back with more force than he expected, and he welcomed it. Her hand brushed over his cheek, leaving a soft, heavenly vibration behind. He pushed her down into the grass, running his hands through her soft curls. The electricity ran stronger, a neverending current that ran through both their bodies and made them one. The flame inside him roared with a heat more pleasant than anything he'd ever felt.

What was this?

Lucas pulled away, unnerved by his own urges and sudden lack of control. Rosie didn't move from her spot lying in the grass. Her chest heaved with deep breaths as she watched him.

"Can you still hear me?" Rosie's voice in his head star-

tled him, and he nodded slowly. She grinned, and a giggle bubbled from her mouth. She covered her face with her hands. *"Oh my God! This is crazy!"*

"How is this possible?" Lucas watched her closely as he projected his question.

She shrugged and giggled again. "Do you feel it, Lucas?" Her eyes bored into his as she asked the question out loud.

"I feel it. I've never felt anything like this. I...I don't...I mean..." Lucas stumbled over his words, having no way to explain the sudden draw he had to her.

The flame inside him—it had never been there before, but now that it was, it felt like a part of him that he couldn't live without.

"Me too." She smiled and reached for his hand.

A knot formed in his stomach. He'd always loved Rosie, but this feeling was so much more. He would do absolutely anything for her.

He'd found a part of himself he'd never known was missing.

SAM FLINCHED AS SIMON UNCEREMONIOUSLY DROPPED the wolf trap onto Sheriff Hill's desk. A deafening *clang* filled the room as the heavy metallic object landed.

After breakfast that morning, Simon had contacted the sheriff about the trap Michael had stepped into last night. Of course, he couldn't tell the entire truth, so he told the sheriff Michael had been walking through the woods and narrowly escaped stepping into it. After the sheriff agreed to a meeting, Simon ordered Sam to come along, telling him, "This is the kind of thing you'll have to take care of one day."

"I want this imbecile arrested, Craig." Simon extended his arm, pointing a finger at Paul Lewis. "Michael could have been killed."

"It's not mine, Simon. How many times do I have to tell you that?" Paul clenched his teeth in barely controlled rage.

"Then why does it have your identification on it?" Simon turned toward Paul, his face reddening in anger.

"I don't know!" Paul raised his shoulders.

"I've had enough of you, Lewis. You're lucky Rosie

doesn't want to press charges against your cretin son, but I have no problem pressing charges against you."

"Mason didn't do anything to your daughter, Simon," Paul seethed. "He said she threw herself at him."

Simon lunged forward, throwing Paul against the wall. Grabbing the man's shirt into his fists, Simon held him against the wall, shaking with rage. Sam couldn't see his father's face from where he was standing, but fear cramped in his stomach as Paul's face morphed into a look of surprised terror. Sam had no doubt that his father's eyes were glowing. He was on the cusp of changing.

"Enough!" Sheriff Hill's shout seemed to get through to Simon, and his tense body visibly relaxed as he stepped away from Paul, whose bulging eyes didn't leave Simon's face. "Simon, I can't arrest Paul. There isn't enough evidence he was actually on your property. But..." The sheriff raised a hand in a placating gesture as Simon spun to face him, his body still tense with fury. Paul's shocked gaze still hadn't left Simon's face. "I can issue a restraining order. If he's caught on your property, he'll be arrested."

"His eyes..." Paul's voice shook as he pointed at Simon. "They were glowing."

"What?" Sheriff Hill looked at Paul like he'd grown a second head.

Paul swallowed as he looked from Simon to the sheriff then back again. "They were glowing. I saw them."

"Are you okay, Paul? Have you been drinking this morning?" The sheriff's confusion turned to annoyance. "Are we going to have a problem? I don't want to throw you in the clink for drinking and driving again."

"This guy is nuts," Simon seethed. "I don't want him anywhere near me or my family."

"All right, Simon." The sheriff reached into his desk and

pulled out some paperwork. "There are some forms and a process to follow, but we'll get it started."

"Whatever," Simon grumbled. "Whatever we have to do."

Sam hid a grin as the worry that they'd been exposed deflated. His dad was good.

TWENTY-TWO
ROSIE

Below the boardwalk in Hanks Hollow, a set of stone stairs descended into the water of Mingan Lake. Rosie sat at one of the tables on the patio outside Miller's Bar and Grill and listened as the water lapped against the stones. Every once in a while, a speedboat would race by, and the gentle lapping would be replaced by loud splashes. The sounds were soothing, and she thought she could spend the entire day sitting there, listening.

"Sorry for the wait, Rosie." Becca grabbed the chair next to Rosie and pulled it out with a loud scraping noise that made her cringe. "We're short-staffed today, so my dad asked me to fill in. We're pretty slow now that the lunch rush is over, so I was finally able to get away."

"It's okay." Rosie shrugged and took a sip of her soda. "I don't have anything planned for the day, and Sam and Lucas said they don't need the car. I'm free all afternoon."

Becca's father owned the popular boardwalk restaurant where they often met and talked. It was Tuesday, two days since the weekend that had altered everything. It had been all Rosie could think about—day and night.

After the euphoric bliss of her first kiss Saturday night, her head was in the clouds until she was brought crashing back to earth when Michael was injured during their run later that evening. She could feel Amos's hate as she healed Michael, and it tore a hole in her.

The next day, when Lucas kissed her again, her whole world shifted. The feelings she had were more intense than anything she'd ever felt in her life. It was more than love, more than anything she could ever have dreamed of experiencing. When she heard his voice in her head, claiming her as his, she had never wanted anything more in her entire life.

They spent every moment together Sunday and Monday. The air between them buzzed. Rosie had known Lucas since they were six, but suddenly, she felt like she'd known him for ten lifetimes.

"So anyway," Becca said as she settled down with a soda and a chef salad. She'd brought one for Rosie, too, but she was too distracted to eat. "Are you going to tell me what the hell happened?"

Rosie looked at her, startled. She hadn't told Becca about Lucas.

Becca stabbed her fork into a bed of lettuce, ham, and ranch dressing. "The only thing anyone saw was Lucas storming off to break Mason's nose and then the two of you leaving in a hurry."

Rosie sighed as she realized Becca was asking about the party. That *horrible* party. It seemed like a lifetime ago. "There isn't much more to tell." She really didn't want to think about that night. "Mason came on to me. Strong."

Rosie swallowed as the memories came flooding back. Her arms pinned to her sides, the feel of his hands pulling up her skirt. "He wouldn't let me go," she said, her voice strained. "I'm not really sure what would have happened if Lucas hadn't come when he did." She was lying. She had a pretty good idea what would have happened.

"Jeez," Becca said, her mouth hanging open. "Do you think he would have—"

"I don't know."

"I guess Lucas must have had a feeling something like that would happen," Becca said, taking a sip of her soda.

Rosie squinted in confusion. "What do you mean?"

Becca raised her eyebrow. "He was shouting at everyone to turn off the music, then he kept asking where Mason took you."

Rosie thought back to that night. She had heard shouting after the music turned off. It must have been Lucas trying to find her.

"He kissed me." Rosie blurted it out then immediately regretted it. Something felt wrong about sharing it with someone else. What she had with Lucas was special...sacred.

"Mason?" Becca sounded baffled. Of course Becca would think Rosie was talking about Mason.

Rosie decided to roll with it. "Yeah," she said as she quickly took a bite of her salad.

Becca's brow furrowed as she eyed Rosie. "I gathered that. It sounds like he wanted more than just a kiss." Her furrowed eyebrows suddenly rose to her hairline as her eyes widened and her mouth formed an O. "You're talking about Lucas!"

Rosie slowly, deliberately swallowed the bite of salad she had been chewing.

"Shut. Up." Becca screamed. "No way!"

Rosie's cheeks grew hot. There was no going back now. "It was perfect." She sighed happily.

"Was it that night? Why the heck didn't you tell me earlier?"

"It wasn't that night. It was this past Saturday." She blushed. "And again on Sunday."

Becca stared at Rosie and shook her head. "You're so lucky. He's so hot."

Rosie's brow crinkled, a territorial growl burning silently in her chest as she resisted an urge to tackle her friend. She took a deep breath as a surge of shock ran through her. Had she actually considered taking Becca down? What the hell was wrong with her?

BECCA AND ROSIE spent the rest of the afternoon wandering in and out of shops on the boardwalk before making their way to the stores on Main Street. Rosie bought some cheese curds and fudge and tried to buy a few shirts. Becca turned up her nose at Rosie's choices and wouldn't let her.

"Honestly, Rosie," she said as she took a shirt from Rosie and returned it to the rack. "You're hopeless. You know that's a boy's shirt, don't you?"

"I like the color," Rosie said, trying to grab at the shirt again. Becca swatted her hand away as she rolled her eyes.

"It's gorgeous today," Becca said, looking up at the sky as they walked out of the store, back into the sunlight.

The street was full of tourists chatting happily as they browsed the shops. It was hard not to feel uplifted by the excited energy of people on vacation.

"I think it's supposed to be like this all week. You want to go out on the pontoon Friday?" Becca asked as she steered them toward the ice cream shop.

Rosie bit the inside of her cheek. That sounded amazing, but Thursday night was a full moon, and the way she felt on days following a full moon tended to be akin to a hangover.

Not many things about werewolf lore were accurate, but the correlation between a full moon and a werewolf change wasn't far off. The phases of the moon affected all creatures to some extent—werewolves and witches were just more aware of the effects and prone to harnessing them. A full moon brought out the wild side in people, and werewolves were no exception.

"I can't," Rosie said with a sigh. "I'm sorry. I have a family thing."

"You always have a family thing," Becca complained.

Rosie was about to apologize—again—for bailing on Becca—again—when her phone buzzed with a new message.

DAD: *Come home now.*

Rosie's stomach somersaulted when she saw the message was from her father.

"I have to go," Rosie said, watching Becca frown in disappointment. "I'm sorry. It's my dad. You know how he is."

"Yeah, yeah," Becca said, waving a hand at her dismissively. "Just try not to be a stranger."

Rosie gave Becca a hug before she ran off toward the Explorer, giving her one final wave over her shoulder.

TWENTY-THREE
ROSIE

"You can't be serious."

"You know I'm always serious, Rose. It's one of the things most people don't like about me." Simon gave Rosie a quick smile. Seated at his desk, he had his hands folded in front of him, and he fiddled his thumbs absently as he spoke. A sigh escaped him as he stood from his chair and moved around to the front of the desk, leaning against it and crossing his arms. "They'll be here tomorrow afternoon."

Rosie knew her father wouldn't have called her home for something small, so she was expecting some sort of bombshell, but this was a meteor. The Council was coming to Hart House to see Rosie. Apparently, they wanted to talk about her future. Her mind went to what her grandma had said about not letting other people run her life.

Easier said than done, Grandma.

"They haven't seen you since you were a pup." Simon sighed. "They are curious, naturally, to see how the world's only known female werewolf is faring."

"So they can decide what to do with me, right?" Rosie crossed her arms. "This sucks, Dad."

She tried not to think about the fact that the Council could very well be rethinking their decision to let her live. While that wasn't likely, the possibility lingered in the air, unspoken.

"I know," he said, nodding as he looked out his office window. "But we don't really have a choice. You know that."

Rosie did know. The United States Werewolf Council had the final say in how werewolves operated in the United States. Fewer than five hundred werewolves lived across the country. Most of them were in Alaska, but a large number of them lived in northern Michigan, Wisconsin, and Minnesota. A few made their homes throughout the northern Rocky Mountain region and the Pacific Northwest. The packs mainly populated areas where regular wolves maintained a natural habitat. Werewolves were good at staying hidden, but if they were going to be seen, it was best to be seen in an area where someone didn't find wolves unusual.

Worldwide, Russia and Canada had the highest volume of regular wolves, so many werewolves made their homes there. A World Council of Werewolves existed in Canada, and it had representation from each country where werewolves resided.

After a few moments of silence, Simon turned to look at Rosie.

"I don't know what they're going to say, Rose." His voice was calm, but the intensity of his fear was palpable. It was fear for her, and it made her queasy. "But whatever it is, we'll deal with it together. I promise."

～

Tension vibrated in the air as Rosie stood with the pack in front of Hart House. The day was beautiful, normally great for being outside, but she would rather have been upstairs, hiding under her bed. Rosie watched a black SUV approach, its tires rolling smoothly over the stamped-concrete driveway. Its tinted windows hid the passengers well, and Rosie averted her gaze when she realized how hard she was trying to stare through them. She didn't want to look like she was gawking.

Three members made up the Council—one from each of the three regions of the United States most heavily populated by werewolves. As the SUV came to a stop, the Council members climbed out, stretching their limbs and focusing their attention on her father as he approached. Rosie tried to guess who was from which region. She knew of them only through stories told to her by Stuart and Simon.

"Simon." One of the three men moved forward, extending his hand, which Simon met with a firm handshake. Polished and professional in a suit with no tie, the man had neatly combed silver hair framing his tanned, wrinkled face.

"Roland," Simon said. "It's been a long time. You look well."

A tense, nervous energy had replaced Simon's usual calm and commanding presence. Rosie knew from stories that Roland represented the Great Lakes region on the Council. He didn't seem very scary. None of them did. She wondered why her father was so nervous.

A second Council member moved forward and shook her father's hand. He looked like a lumberjack. His tall, beefy frame and squared, broad shoulders made Rosie's father look small in comparison. He wore a flannel shirt and jeans and sported a full beard.

"Jagger," Simon greeted the lumberjack. "It's good to see you again."

Jagger represented Alaska on the Council, which meant the third man greeting her father was Garrett. As the newest and youngest member of the Council, he represented the Pacific Northwest region. He wore a blue button-up shirt and khaki slacks. He was handsome, with thick, unruly brown hair and a rugged five o'clock shadow.

The Council members turned their attention to Rosie, and Lucas tensed beside her. She brushed her fingers over his hand, sending a soothing vibe his way.

Roland was the one who spoke first, and when he approached Rosie, she tensed as she felt something sinister in his energy. Resentment, maybe. The sensation was similar to what she often felt from Amos, though much less intense. She suddenly understood why her father seemed nervous, and she started to feel it too.

"Rose Hart," Roland said in greeting.

Rosie smiled at him but didn't say anything. What could she say?

"Don't be worried, kid," Jagger said with an amused grin. "We're not here to kill you."

She realized she was probably wearing her fear on her face. She'd never been good at masking her emotions.

They moved inside to the large living room, where two brown leather couches sat on either side of an enormous stone fireplace. The couches, along with several armchairs around the room, supplied adequate seating, and everyone sat except Roland, who moved to the fireplace, resting a hand on the mantel.

"I'll cut right to the chase," Roland said, leveling a

hard stare at Rosie. "I'm old-fashioned. I've been around a long time, and in my day, women served one purpose in the werewolf world. Just one. If werewolves could multiply without women, I would have no need for them. The idea of a female werewolf is ludicrous. I voted to have you killed when you were a baby, but I was outvoted."

Rosie's pulse quickened. She'd been assured they weren't there to kill her, but she had the distinct feeling that Roland would like nothing more than to end her right here and now.

"I've been outvoted again," Roland said, glancing toward the other Council members. "Times are changing. As women have risen up in the human world, it's made the newest generations of werewolves soft."

"Perhaps one of us should have spoken instead," Garrett cut in, shooting an irritated glance at Roland. "Times *are* changing. While we are not averse to executions when someone threatens our existence, the Council isn't in the business of killing without cause." He gave Rosie a reassuring smile. Dimples dotted each cheek, making him look young and sweet.

Jagger leaned forward and rested his elbows on his knees. "Our purpose is to uphold the laws that were put in place to keep our existence safe and secret," he said. "I'm well aware of the fear that follows us. It's not unfounded. We don't have many laws, but rest assured if you break those laws, we will come for you. The werewolf guard under our command are trained to kill, and they're good at what they do." He glanced toward Roland before he continued, "We have no laws that pertain to female werewolves because there has never been a female werewolf. I can't help but think you are here for a reason. I don't know what it is. But I'm not about to snuff out your existence before we have the chance to find out."

"We're embracing women in a way that hasn't been done in the past," Garrett said. "In Washington, some of our packs have invited the women who have mothered our werewolves into our homes. They live among us, helping us to raise our young."

An irritated sound came from the corner of the room, and Rosie looked over at Amos, who had his face turned up in disgust.

Garrett noticed and addressed him directly. "I know it isn't a popular practice, but we are not breaking any laws. We keep the women with us. They don't leave, and there is no threat to the secrecy of our existence."

"What if one of them decides to take off?" Amos spat. "Women can't be trusted. A spurned woman will spread the word the first chance she gets."

"We have had only one woman who tried to leave," Garrett said. "The women in our packs understand that they are bound to us. Leaving the pack means death."

"W-what happened to her?" Rosie's voice shook, and she regretted asking the question immediately.

Garrett gave her a hard stare, and for the first time, she felt afraid of him. "We hunted her down and ripped out her throat," he said bluntly. "I consider myself a compassionate person, but my compassion ends when our kind is threatened."

"And that's why he's on the Council," Jagger said with a grin.

Roland rolled his eyes dramatically. "Oh please."

"What does that mean for Rosie?" Sam chimed in impatiently.

"Sam!" Simon hissed.

All three Council members looked at Sam.

"Your future alpha, I presume?" Roland asked slowly, his eyebrow raised.

"My apologies," Simon said. "He's still learning."

"See that he learns his place," Roland said with a deadly grin, "or I'll teach him myself."

"Enough with the dramatics, Roland," Jagger said, rolling his eyes. He turned his stare back to Rosie. "As Garrett said, we're not in the business of killing werewolves simply for existing. Your life is not in danger. At least not from us."

"But that does leave your future in question," Garrett said. "We've spent many hours discussing the impact you could have on the future of all werewolves. This was a discussion that needed input from everyone."

"You mean..." Rosie's voice was barely a whisper, and she stopped, not sure she could manage a full sentence.

"We spoke with the World Council," Jagger said. "We met for several days, actually."

"Waste of time," Roland growled. "They're just a bunch of superstitious old fools. Babbling on about gods and Chosen ones."

Rosie's sharp intake of breath was a knee-jerk reaction, and it didn't go unnoticed.

"So you've heard about the gods." Jasper eyed Rosie before turning toward Simon. "Funny. I wouldn't have pegged you as a believer."

Simon shook his head. "My father told me a little, but he said it was just an old story."

"The story of the gods and the Chosen is documented in some of our old journals, but the story stopped being told generations ago." Stuart spoke quietly. "No one believes it."

"Many do believe it." Jasper turned his gaze back to

Rosie. "And they believe that you were sent here for a reason. Maybe to make up for the fact that the werewolves were abandoned by the witches so long ago. Maybe you're the start of a new generation of Chosen."

Rosie bit her lip again. She'd gotten a different version of the story from her grandmother. Apparently, the werewolves and the witches remembered the past a little differently. The werewolves didn't seem to like the witches any more than the witches liked the werewolves. What would happen if they found out she was part witch?

"They're crazy," Roland said in a low growl. "Your existence can be perceived as a threat."

"Or as an opportunity," Garrett said, staring at Roland intensely. "It all depends on whether you're ready to embrace something new, or intent on holding onto the past."

"There was quite the difference of opinion on the matter." Jagger sighed as a wave of exhausted frustration came from him. "But in the end, those who are ready to embrace the future far outnumbered those who...aren't." He glanced at Roland, who rolled his eyes and stared at the fireplace.

"You're young, Rose," Garrett said. "We hope there will be some time before you're ready to...procreate."

Rosie's cheeks heated, and she wanted to crawl under the floorboards.

"When you are, there should be measures in place to ensure that what is brought into this world is..." Garrett trailed off, looking like he was trying to choose his next word carefully. "Suitable."

"So you want to pimp her off to the best bull in the herd," Sam said, his face pinched in disgusted anger.

A vicious growl sounded before Sam was quickly pinned to the floor under the substantial weight of a very pissed-off werewolf. Rosie was sure the werewolf who charged was Roland, but he was still standing next to the fireplace, an amused smile on his face. She was surprised to find that Garrett was no longer sitting on the couch.

The werewolf on Sam's chest snarled, his teeth inches from Sam's throat.

"Stop!" Rosie screamed, jumping to her feet. "Please!"

"Garrett!" Jagger yelled. "Enough!"

Garrett changed back to human form, but he continued to pin Sam to the floor with his large, muscular arms. His jaw twitched, and his face reddened in rage. "This is not a joke to us, *pup*," he seethed. "I will not be disrespected again."

Sam nodded once, staring up at Garrett with wide eyes.

Garrett stood, eyes still on Sam. "My apologies, Simon," he said. "I meant no offense, changing in your territory."

Rosie noticed her father was standing. His glowing eyes told her he was seconds away from changing too. If Garrett hadn't backed down, her father would have attacked, which could have spelled death for more than one person in the room. Her stomach turned.

"We are all on edge," Jagger said calmly. "We spent several days in intense discussion with leaders from around the globe."

"Sam," Simon said, not taking his eyes off Garrett. "You owe an apology to the Council for your disrespect."

Sam stood from the floor, his head bowed. "I apologize," he said. "I meant no disrespect."

"Yes, you did," Garrett said quickly, pinning him with a piercing stare.

Sam looked away. "I did," he admitted, making Rosie's stomach flutter nervously. "But I was wrong. I apologize."

"You will make a good alpha one day, kid," Garrett said.

"But before you do, you need to learn when to keep a lid on it."

Garrett looked at the floor where his clothes lay in a torn heap. Then he looked at Rosie with a sheepish grin. Rosie's cheeks heated as she tried not to stare at the naked, godlike stranger in front of her.

"Your brother's eloquence could use some work, but he wasn't wrong," Garrett said.

Rosie glanced at Sam then back at Garrett. Her pulse quickened, and her mouth went dry.

"We want to be sure that any offspring you bring into this world is fathered by another werewolf." As he spoke, Jagger's posture became rigid, and his focus narrowed on her. She felt a shift—a nervous awareness that her world was once again on the cusp of significant change. "You will mate with an alpha."

EPILOGUE

His black paws barely made a sound as he crept quietly through the brush. In the distance, Hart House beckoned to him. Home. His home. His birthright. Hart blood ran through his veins. Descended from generations of Hart men who knew what tradition and loyalty meant. His body thrummed with a need to be there. He knew every rock, every tree. He'd grown up there.

Tradition. It was what kept werewolves alive for centuries. When they were abandoned by witches—by *women*—they learned to adapt. His father's words echoed through his head as he recalled the stories from long ago. Werewolves were men. *Only* men. They rallied together and survived.

Now, a new generation wanted to change things...to rewrite history...to bring women into the pack. Into *their* pack. A female werewolf...walking on *their* land. Tainting *their* soil. Sickening.

While the female werewolf enjoyed herself in his home, he was left out in the cold. A gaping hole had replaced the space within, where his pack used to reside, now a frigid, endless pit of despair. The loneliness nagged at him every moment of every day—like having a part of the body missing. No longer able to breathe right...couldn't sleep...couldn't eat. Nothing was right anymore.

Simon had banished him to a hell unlike any he could have ever imagined.

Roaming from town to town, trying to find a way to live with the sorrow and rage that burned inside...It drove him nuts on the best days. On the worst days, when the moon was full, horror struck. He had to be careful not to be seen. Trying to find a wooded area where a pack didn't have territory marked was nearly impossible. Cowering in the trees, he would try to hold off as long as he could, but his mind wasn't his own, and the change always came. His control slipped away with his sanity. How many times had he found himself alone and naked in the middle of nowhere? When he wandered aimlessly to the nearest town, the authorities locked him up and questioned where he came from. He couldn't articulate an answer.

Back to the loony bin. He'd been in and out of so many of them. They pumped him so full of drugs the urge to change left him, and he would find a moment of peace even if he was so out of it that he couldn't wipe his own chin.

Thank God Amos had found him.

He heard the other wolf coming, and he turned slowly. He could barely see the outline of the sleek black coat in the shadows. His eyes narrowed as he watched Amos step into the moonlight.

"*Frank.*" Amos's clinical tone irritated him as much in telepathy as it did when he heard it out loud. It reminded him of the hospitals—the doctors...the nurses. "*What took you so long to get here? I called you days ago.*"

Their call to each other could stretch farther than any

distance they'd traveled. No matter how far apart, they'd always been able to hear each other. Though not able to hold a full conversation, they could hear a call for help. A call to come. A twin thing, most likely, but they'd never told anyone about it. Their little secret. Frank had spent years calling to Amos. It had taken his brother so long to answer.

"I was deep in Beckett territory, and their pack went out for a run." Frank turned his gaze back to Hart House. The lights in the bedrooms started to flick off as the pack members settled into bed for the evening. *"I think Marcus spotted me."*

"Dammit, Frank." Amos growled. *"I told you to stay in Hart territory, where I can cover your scent. They've already spotted you in Cramer territory. Why the hell can't you stay put?"*

A low growl rumbled in Frank's throat. *"I've been cowering for years, Amos. I need to run. The itch to belong to the pack is still there. It makes me restless. I can't sit still."*

"Have you been taking your medication?" Amos paced in front of Frank, his lip curling. *"It will only work to lessen your anxiety if you take it."*

"I've been taking it, Amos." Frank turned to his brother, his mirror image. *"It helps, but the itch is still there. What did good ol' William do when he smelled me? Does Simon suspect it's me?"*

"This isn't a game, Frank." Amos stopped his pacing and bared his teeth. *"I managed to convince Simon you were dead years ago. I told him I went against his orders and kept tabs on you and that you died in the psych ward. But now that a rogue is out there, smelling like one of the pack, I'm sure he suspects I lied."*

"Good." Frank raised his chin. *"I want him to be scared. Him and that little abomination he brought into this world."*

"The younger generation doesn't know you exist. Simon ordered us to keep it quiet. The only ones in the pack left who know about you are Stuart and I."

"Still...I gave the little brat something to be scared of. Even gave her a little scar to remember me by."

"It almost didn't work as planned," Amos growled. *"She tried to keep it a secret. Thank goodness Lucas spilled the beans."*

"I still don't understand why we can't just kill her."

"We've been over this, you idiot. It can't get back to us. If the Council finds out it was us, we're dead. We need to pin it on someone else. Paul Lewis is perfect. He and Simon have been feuding for years." Amos looked toward Hart House then leveled a stare at Frank. *"Are you sure they didn't smell you?"*

"I doused myself in aftershave and stuffed my pockets with chew. No way they smelled me."

"They better not have. You know we smell the same. If they smell you, they'll think it's me."

That was the thing about werewolf twins...they shared the same smell as well as physical appearances.

"Relax. No one is going to smell anything past that stinky aftershave. I've been hunting with Paul and left my gear at his house just like you told me to do."

"How are you keeping yourself disguised? I've seen the beard. You'll need more than that to hide the fact that you look just like me."

"I never go anywhere without my shades and hat on. No one has seen my eyes."

"We need to act soon. The Council wants the little harlot to mate with an alpha. We can't let that happen. I've started planting rumors. I told one of the Cramers that Rose's mother was a witch and that she performs witchcraft right here at

Hart House. Made him promise to keep it a secret. Of course, he won't. Rumors will spread quietly, and no one will know where it started. As long as it doesn't get traced back to us, no one will suspect anything."

"When do I get to kill her?" Frank salivated at the thought of running a blade across her throat.

"Soon. We need to get Paul and Simon at each other's throats. After you kill her, Simon will lose it. When rumors about her spread, Simon will have to answer to the Council for his secrets and lies. If he isn't executed, he'll at least be stripped of his title as alpha. His boy, Samuel, isn't up to the task of taking his place. Kid is as irresponsible as they come. I'll be able to take over. And then I'll bring you back into the pack, brother. I promise."

The Hanks Hollow Series Continues...

<u>Witch in a Wolf Den</u>

<u>Lost in Hanks Hollow</u>

<u>When Witches Wake</u>

THANK YOU

Dear Reader,

THANK YOU for reading *Moon Over Hanks Hollow*! These characters have become such a big part of my world, and I really hope you enjoyed meeting them. If you liked the story, please consider leaving a review on <u>Amazon</u> or <u>Goodreads</u>. Reviews and ratings help me so much, and I would be so grateful for the support!

For updates, follow me on Facebook, TikTok, or Instagram, and be sure to sign up for my newsletter!

https://linktr.ee/rachellekampen

https://www.facebook.com/rachellekampen

https://www.tiktok.com/@rachellekampen

https://www.instagram.com/rachellekampen/

ACKNOWLEDGMENTS

First and foremost, I want to thank my family. Aaron, you have put up with so much from me, and your love and support has been unending. I couldn't get through a single day of my life without you. Annie, you are the light of my life. Your encouragement and praise make me feel like I can move mountains. I am so lucky to be your mom. Caleb, your humor, kindness, and sense of responsibility bring so much to our crazy little world, and I'm so lucky to have you in my life.

I want to thank my friend and fellow author, Gina Sturino. Your advice, encouragement, and friendship have been a monumental support system for me. Thank you so much.

Thank you to my friend Amanda. Our daily text conversations keep me laughing when everything else in life feels overwhelming.

Thank you to Jessica Fraser and all of the beta readers, artists, and editors who have helped me along the way.

ABOUT THE AUTHOR

Rachelle Kampen grew up on a farm in southern Wisconsin with three brothers and two sisters. In a rural setting with no cable television or internet, options for things to do were limited, so she read—a lot.

Though she's been writing stories from the time she learned to pen a sentence, she didn't take the leap into publishing until she started writing the Hanks Hollow series. The beloved characters and unique world of Hanks Hollow unite some of Wisconsin's fun quirks with a magical paranormal adventure.

She lives outside Madison, Wisconsin with her husband, daughter, two dogs, and two cats. Even now, with cable and internet at her fingertips, she loves a good book to pass the time.

You can find author Rachelle Kampen at:
    https://linktr.ee/rachellekampen
    https://www.facebook.com/rachellekampen
    https://www.tiktok.com/@rachellekampen
    https://www.instagram.com/rachellekampen/

9 798986 075204